Also by Robert Newton Peck

Robert Newton Peck

illustrations
by
Charles Robinson

Alfred A. Knopf 🐕 New York

Library of Congress Cataloging-in-Publication Data

Peck, Robert Newton.
Soup 1776 / by Robert Newton Peck ; illustrated by Charles Robinson.
p.   cm.
Summary: Rob is caught up in his friend Soup's plan to help their town of
Learning, Vermont, celebrate the Fourth of July with a suitable pageant that sets
the record straight about several of the town's citizens.
ISBN 0-679-87320-1 (trade) — ISBN 0-679-97320-6 (lib. bdg.)
[1. City and town life—Fiction. 2. Vermont—Fiction. 3. Humorous stories.]
I. Robinson, Charles, 1931– ill.   II. Title.
PZ7.P339Soaag   1995
[Fic]—dc20   94-23879
Manufactured in the United States of America
10 9 8 7 6 5 4 3 2 1

Chapter 1

"Run," said Soup.

"Why do we have to run?" I asked him.

"Look behind us, Rob."

I looked.

At once, I shifted gears to full throttle. Our only hope was to make it to school, our haven of safety. Because, hot on our high-flying heels, we saw Janice Riker!

BANG.

The sudden sound, very close and very loud, warned me that Janice, who was Vermont's version of King Kong, was armed with a slingshot. Some kids fired acorns or horse chestnuts. Janice shot cherry bombs. This is not a firecracker. A cherry bomb explodes with the force of two inches of a stick of dynamite.

So we doubled our speed. For good reason.

Long ago, Soup and I had decided that if Janice Riker was drowning, we'd throw her a rock. There wasn't a kid in Learning who dared to confront her. Not even Eddy Tacker, the toughest of all boys, who chewed tobacco. Janice didn't. She chewed cigars. When lit.

Soup and I, panting heavily, final reached our little one-room schoolhouse. Miss Kelly, luckily, was already there, primly seated at her desk.

"Luther and Robert," she said with a welcoming smile. "It's so nice that you're here early on this beautiful June day."

We also smiled. "Good morning, Miss Kelly."

Ten minutes later, all twenty-eight of us were seated. Soup Vinson and I shared a bench, a desk, and an open history book. Our teacher stood before us, pointer in hand, tapping a wall map of what I presumed was Asia or some other South American country.

"Here," said Miss Kelly, "is England."

I already knew that Learning was in Vermont, part of New England. So, I decided, it wasn't necessary to overdo attention. Instead, my eyes drifted to a more succulent subject.

Norma Jean Bissell.

She sat in regal splendor, the prettiest girl in the school. History retreated as romance advanced.

Up front, Miss Kelly was lecturing about independence, little of which could capture my rapture. Instead, I was admiring the princess of my passion, Norma Jean Bissell, girl goddess. Only yards

2

away. My soul throbbed like a happy hemorrhoid.

"Norma Jean," I sighed in prayer.

My devotions were abruptly interrupted by Luther Wesley Vinson, whose elbow jabbed my ribs.

"Beware," said Soup. "We guys are merely *kids*. But girls are already *small women*."

I ignored him. Instead, I looked at *her*, Norma Jean Bissell, the girl who liked me. Even though she'd remarked that I usual smelled of *cow*.

"Independence," whispered Soup.

"Huh?"

"Rob, you'll lose it if you ever get married. You shall walk the Last Mile to the altar. Before you regain consciousness, you'll become the lowest form of humanity."

"And what's that?"

"A *husband*." Soup paused for a mirthless grin. "Girls," he said, "are after only *one thing*."

Miss Kelly continued. "England," she said, "is historically called our mother country. Why? Because our culture and customs, even our government, are basically British. The English settlers came to America for freedom. And, of course, for their first edible food."

Norma Jean Bissell touched her flaxen hair.

"Soup," I whispered, "do you think Miss Kelly would notice if you and I switched places so I could sit closer to Norma Jean?"

Soup sighed. "Rob . . . she'd notice."

"Now maybe," I told Soup, "being Norma Jean's husband wouldn't be so horrible."

"Robert Newton Peck, unless you watch your step, you are about to walk the Plank of Peril. Life, old sport, is a diving board. A bridegroom is blindfolded upon a high dive. Far below, marriage is looming as an empty pool. Except for a downward drain to oblivion."

However, as I was digesting my pal's morbid morsel of warning, Norma Jean's eyes met mine, her lids limpid with longing. As she smiled, my hastening heart was clanging like a slot machine's jackpot.

"A *wife*," Soup was saying, "is a girl's way of saying the *B* word. Boss! Marriage, as I view it, is legal tyranny."

"Tyranny!" Miss Kelly raised her voice, making me jump. "That's what Patrick Henry, a patriot, called taxation without representation. And," she added, "taxation *for* representation could be worse."

As I jumped, my knee cracked the bottom of our desk, and it hurt like holy heck. I had an urge to yell a lot more than "tyranny." But then something else happened.

A car honked.

Walking to the window, Miss Kelly looked out and turned back to us. "Class," she announced, "we

4

have a visitor. So, as hosts and hostesses, let's display our best manners."

Without a knock, our caller opened the door and exploded into our schoolroom. As usual, she was dressed entirely in white, because this XL (extra-large) lady's job was serving as our county nurse. She was also our teacher's longtime friend.

"Howdy, troops!" blared Miss Boland.

"Welcome," said Miss Kelly, who gave us all a slight nod to prompt our reply.

"Good morning, Miss Boland," we all chorused.

"News," said our nurse. "Have I got news. Yesterday, I drove my Hoover to Thurgood. They're planning a celebration next month for the Fourth of July. A pageant, costumes and music and muskets, fifes and drums, to commemorate Thurgood's famous historical event. That's not all. Folks in Pratt Falls and Mill Creek and North Southby are doing likewise."

"My," said Miss Kelly, "that really *is* news."

"Back in 1776," said Miss Boland, "each one of those tiny hamlets managed to muster a militia, take aim, and spook off the British redcoats. So, to celebrate our upcoming July fourth, they're all throwing pageants."

Miss Kelly said, "Good. Which one should we attend?"

"None," said Miss Boland, fists clenched.

"Why not?"

5

"Because," our nurse said, "all this celebrating and play acting got me thinking."

Miss Boland paused. Then, with a sudden upward whip of her right arm, she saluted our flag, snapping us all to attention. As she marched around the room, knees high, her starched white nurse's uniform crackled with enthusiasm.

At last she halted.

"Here's my idea," she said. "*We're* doing a pageant too. Right here in Learning. Those other towns can't celebrate more patriotically than *we* can." She faced Miss Kelly. "What an opportunity to drench our youngsters in a dandy dose of drama."

Glancing down at the textbook that lay open in front of Soup and me, *Hotbeds of History*, I tried to muffle a groan of doom. History wasn't my favorite form of fun. The college professor who'd written our history book, Dr. P. H. Dee, had done so by using his patented Bore & Yawn System, assisted by the Federal Bureau of Dusty Documents. Reading his text was almost as thrilling as opening night at a grammar fair.

"Now," said Miss Boland, her eyes fired with fervor, "*we* shall put on a pageant, about the historical event that happened here in Learning."

"What was it?" asked Norma Jean Bissell.

"I forgot." She turned to Miss Kelly. "But history's always been one of your hobbies. What *did* happen here? Wasn't it some sort of a battle?"

Miss Kelly nodded. "But . . . "

"Golly," said Miss Boland, "I hope it'll sound as rousing as Mill Creek Charge . . . or North Southby's Advance. We ought to noodle up a fancier name than Thurgood's Triumph. After all, our revered first settler was a war hero named Learning." Making a face, our nurse scratched her head. "By the way, what in the deuce *was* Mr. Learning's first name?"

Miss Kelly answered the question.

"Disability."

"Hey, that's right," Soup mumbled into my ear. "You know. In the park, that's the name on his statue. Yet it's hard to read."

"How come?" I asked Soup.

"Pigeons," he said. "But, once after a hard rain, I saw the name on our granite Minuteman. It was Disability Learning."

"And so far, so good," Miss Boland was saying. "We'll use Mr. Learning's victory over the British redcoats as a central theme for our pageant."

Miss Kelly said, "It wasn't a victory."

Arching her eyebrows in dismay, Miss Boland asked, "It wasn't? Of course it was. How do they record it in our history books?"

Our teacher responded with a sad sigh.

"Disability's Disaster."

Chapter 2

"Today," said Soup, "we try it."

"Maybe we shouldn't," I told my pal while studying the printed sign on the fence.

Soup sighed. "What would Norma Jean Bissell think, were she to suspect Rob Peck of being a spineless ninny?"

We were walking home from school. But I was recalling what Mama had repeatedly told me. Almost every day. Yet, there we stood, staring at the sign that was printed in big letters that were blacker than midnight:

DANGER—KEEP OUT

"Here," said Soup, locking his hands above his bent knees, "I'll boost you over the fence. Rob, remember this. A boy's dream is doing once what men do all the time." Soup grinned. "So let's do it."

I didn't want to do it. For good reason.

"*Never*," my mother had often warned me, "go anywhere *near* old Mr. Wacko's meadow."

Soup's mother, believe it or not, had voiced a similar precaution in almost those exact words. "You *know*," added Mrs. Vinson, "what runs loose in his pasture."

We sure knew.

Looking through the fence into the tiny one-acre meadow, I saw what even the bravest boys were afraid of. There she stood, ears back, staring at Soup and me. Crazy Horse. Both of us could easily see that Crazy Horse wasn't a horse at all. She was a mule. Nobody in his right mind would own such an animal. No one, except . . . Mr. Insanity Wacko.

"Up you go," said Soup.

"This is a dumb idea," I told him.

"No, it isn't. Have you got your carrot?"

Touching my shirt pocket, I felt it. Early this morning, I'd snapped the carrot Soup had given me into three short logs, so it wouldn't show in school, to quell the qualms and queries of Miss Kelly.

"Yep. I got it."

"Well, let's get going. There's nothing to fear. Mules love carrots. And anybody who offers one. Nobody's ever been able to tame Crazy Horse. If we do it, we'll be heroes."

"Okay," I sighed. "But you're coming with me."

"Of course. I'll be behind you all the way. Would I lie?" Soup asked, his blue eyes widening into sincerity, as though he were selling me a used car. With no engine.

9

"Then," I said, "why don't *you* go first?"

Soup moaned.

"Rob, we've already discussed all this. After all, I brought you the carrot. For free. So it's *your* turn to contribute. Don't ask *me* to handle it *all*."

Placing my right foot into Soup's interlaced fingers, I copped one more glance through the fence. Crazy Horse eyed me with unwelcoming suspicion.

"Ready?" asked Soup.

"No, not really."

"Show her the carrot. That might brighten her disposition."

"Here," I said, waving a modest length of home-grown vegetable. "Here it is, Crazy Horse."

"Now," ordered Soup, "straighten your leg. No! Not that one. Brace the leg I'm holding."

As I braced, Soup grunted, lifted, and tossed me over the barbed-wire fence. Well, almost over. During my descent, I heard a *rip*, feeling my pants snag.

I landed.

"You dropped your carrot," said Soup.

At the moment, I didn't honest care. Crazy Horse seemed not to be interested in food. Whipping her tail, she pawed the earth with a hoof. And then brayed.

HEEEEEEEEE HAWWW.

"See?" said Soup. "She's afraid."

"Are you coming? You promised."

"Rob, don't panic. I'm right behind you."

"Yes, but you're *outside*. I'm *in*."

"This," Soup told me, "is hardly the time to bring up some pesky geographical technicality."

Crazy Horse took a step toward me. Then another.

"She's coming!" I yelped. Fear was surging through me like spit through a kazoo.

"Quick, show her the carrot," Soup told me.

"I don't care about a carrot. I'm caring about me."

Bending over, I felt for the carrot log that I'd dropped, keeping my eyes fixed on Mr. Wacko's advancing mule.

Soup giggled. "There's a hole in your pants."

Great, I was thinking. How could I have allowed good old Luther Vinson to talk me into such a mess?

Crazy Horse stopped, kicked her rear hoofs high in the air, brayed again, and then trotted in my direction.

"She looks tame," said Soup.

Not to me, she didn't.

"Whatever you do, Rob, try not to frighten her."

"Frighten *her*?"

To me, Crazy Horse didn't appear frightened at all. Not in the least. Her attitude seemed to be ferocity. If only I had listened to my mother. Or to Soup's mother.

As the mule moved closer, she stopped. Her long ears flopped forward as though she expected me to say something.

"Care for a carrot?" I asked in a puny voice.

"Throw it to her," Soup suggested. "She'll eat it."

"Yeah," I said, "and maybe me for dessert."

Nevertheless, I hurled a hunk of Soup's carrot to Crazy Horse. And received quite a surprise. Ears back, she reared up high, boxing the air with a front hoof. Then, with her forelegs down, bucked twice.

She brayed again.

"Soup," I whispered, "Crazy Horse didn't like it when I threw the carrot at her. Not a bit."

"No," said Soup, "she sure didn't. Robert, you don't seem to have much of a way with animals."

"Look for a hole in the fence," I told him.

"Why? So I can come in?"

"No, you idiot. So I can get *out*."

"Move to your left, Rob."

I moved sideways, like a cautious crab, aiming my eyes at Crazy Horse and wondering what her next move might be. She inched toward me again.

"Help," I heard myself yelp.

"Rob," said Soup, "I think the mule likes you. Look how she's coming to you. Try giving her the rest of the carrot."

"Forget feeding her," I howled. "All I want to do is escape. Find me a hole, and hurry. Now. *Now*, you simpleton."

"Here's one."

"Where?"

"In your pants."

"And," I growled at Soup, "in your *head*."

"Keep moving to your left, Rob."

I drifted left.

The mule moved straight ahead.

"Quick," said Soup. "I'm stretching up a flimsy strand of wire so you can slip through."

Ducking low, lying on meadow grass, I started headfirst into the opening. Halfway through, I felt something holding me back. "My pants are caught on the barbed wire."

"Never mind your pants," Soup said. "I can't hold this prickly fence much longer. Loosen your belt."

"Why?"

"You'll have to leave your pants in the pasture."

"Are you nuts? I can't go home without pants."

"Hurry," said Soup. "She's getting close."

Loosening my belt, I crawled to safety through the gap in the fence. Panting, I lay on my belly between Soup's feet.

"Rob," said Soup, "I realize it's June. Summer and all. But you really ought to consider wearing some underwear. If anyone sees you naked from the waist down, they'll recognize you and maybe tell your mother."

He let go of the wire.

"Help me get my pants, Soup."

"Okay, but you'd better stay there in the tall weeds. Whatever you do, you can't stand up. You're buck naked."

"Get my pants!"

Soup was silent for several seconds.

"Are you getting them?" I asked him.

"Well, I tried. But there now seems to be somewhat of a small problem. Crazy Horse got there before I could."

"She *what?*"

"The mule's got your pants in her mouth."

Rolling over, parting the weeds with my hands, I looked and saw exactly what I feared I'd see. There stood Crazy Horse, holding my pants in her teeth. Then she slowly backed away from the fence.

"Hey," I hollered, "bring those back!"

HEE HAWWWWW.

Crazy Horse seemed to be laughing at me. So was Soup. They both chuckled fit to bust. But they weren't the only ones. I heard a third laugh. It wasn't Soup's or the mule's. It was somebody else.

Turning, I saw who it was, standing only a few feet away from the two of us. I guessed who, because I knew everyone else in Learning. This was someone whom I hadn't seen in years.

Mr. Insanity Wacko.

Chapter 3

He kept laughing.

Mr. Wacko was a little old man with a wrinkled face and white hair. Yet never had I seen a person laugh so hard. And so long. He final quit for a breather.

"Boys," he said, "I gotta bless the both of ya. Ain't seen anything funnier than you two clowns in over twenty years."

"Are you angry?" Soup asked.

"Shucks, no, I ain't angry. I watched the whole business. When I seen ya brung a carrot for my mule, I figured right off that you wasn't bad boys."

The way Mr. Wacko looked at me, then at Soup, made me like him. Everyone in town claimed he was nothing but an ornery old hermit. Yet a lot of his critics rarely cracked a smile.

"My name's Wacko," he said. "And with a name like that, a feller just has to keep a sense of humor."

As he talked, I pulled off my shirt, tying it around my lower body, knotting the sleeves so I'd appear halfway decent.

"Some kids," Mr. Wacko said, "throw stones at my mule. But I can tell by your faces that you're not unkind. You rascals look sort of hot and sweated. How'd ya like to put yourselfs outside a sip of cider?"

"Gee," said Soup, "that'd be swell."

I nodded. "It sure would."

We followed Mr. Wacko to his shack. It looked as tumbledown as its owner, but neither Soup nor I was about to bother.

"Wait outside," he told us. He entered, then returned with a cider jug. "Don't worry," Mr. Wacko said, "it ain't hard cider. This'n is apple sweet. And cool. I store it deep in my earth bin."

Soup took a swig. So did I. It was about the best cider that had ever dribbled down my chin. We both thanked our jovial host.

"Aren't *you* going to have any?" Soup asked.

"Nope. Gives me gas. I just sort of keep it handy, for visitors." He sighed. "But I don't git so many of those. I'm olden. Close to one hundred years."

Soup's face brightened. "Say," he said, "I bet you remember everything that's ever happened here in our village."

"Me? Not quite. Yet when I was a tadpole, younger than you two, my old grandpappy used to tell me *history*. He was here in 1776. Back when the British redcoats come. Fact is, he was a close sidekick to a fine and noble gentleman by the name of Ability Learning."

Soup and I looked at each other. Perhaps he was now wondering, as I was, if we'd learn the truth about the founder of our town.

"Yup," said Mr. Wacko, as if reading our minds, "it was Ability Learning who saved a few dozen lives. As leader of the local militia, he realized that our local New England patriots were little more than young lads with squirrel muskets. My grandpappy was one of them. And it'd be folly to charge 'em against the British regulars, who were well trained and heavily armed."

"How did the Disability name come about?" Soup asked.

"According to Grandpap, there was a local politician who envied Ability Learning. His name was Mr. Dee. As I recall, he had several sons, all named after musical instruments. There was Fife and Bagpipe and Drum. The old man's name was Fiddle."

I flinched. "His first name was Fiddle?"

Mr. Wacko nodded. "Yup. It was Fiddle D. Dee."

"Honest?" I asked.

"Yup. Grandpap even recalled the tribe of Indians that hunted here, when the Yankee colonists first arrived."

"What tribe was it, Mr. Wacko?" asked Soup.

"The Wahooligans."

I held my breath. Listening to old Mr. Wacko talk was a lot more exciting than wading through the lifeless pages in *Hotbeds of History.*

"Mr. Wacko," I asked, "what happened in 1776?"

"A plenty. The redcoats were coming, on their way to Fort Ticonderoga. And the Wahooligan Indians came to wahoo a warning. And they also brought a peace pipe."

"Was there a battle?" Soup asked.

"Well, there was sort of a battle scene. Nobody got kilt. This was possible a disappointment to the Dee clan, being out for blood. So they called Mr. Learning's caution disastrous . . . Disability's Disaster. Even recorded as such on paper. Years ago, I used to serve as the village historian. And I wrote about 1776 like it actual happened, until the truth twisters didn't want reality. They tried to make me tamper with the truth. The politicians called it *correcting.*"

"But you didn't back down?" I asked.

Before answering, our host gestured to a hand-made bench, so Soup and I could sit and rest easy. Mr. Wacko sat under a maple tree, on a chair cut from a barrel.

"Did I change it? No. I wouldn't falsify the facts," Mr. Wacko told us. "The Chamber of Commerce got me fired. Lost my job. Some of our town's bigwig lawyers claimed I was insane, even though my real name is Sanity. So I become a hermit. That's me. Old Insanity Wacko, who lives all alone and keeps a mule named Crazy Horse."

Soup looked at me and winked. From the expression on his face, I knew right away that something was forming in his mind.

There I sat, wearing only a shirt where my trousers ought to be. And more, in the company of two other oddities: Old Mr. Insanity Wacko and Luther Wesley Vinson. I smelled trouble. Soup, I knew, was about to hatch one of his idiotic ideas. Sure enough, the egg Soup called a head began to crack. A plan was about to be born.

Soup snapped his fingers.

Then, looking my way, he spoke only one word.

"Pageant."

"Come again?" asked Mr. Wacko.

"Mr. Wacko," said my pal, jumping to his feet. "You may not realize it yet, but Learning is about to celebrate 1776. All over again. Better yet, sir, do it the way you claim it rightly happened."

"You don't say."

Soup nodded. "Miss Boland's come up with a theme for the Fourth of July pageant. But, as I figure it, Miss Boland knows a lot about health. But not history. Therefore, somebody's got to write a script."

"Who?" I asked.

Soup grinned.

"Oh," he said with a shrug, "nobody in particular. But whoever takes on the job could play one peach of a prank on those mean people who got you fired, Mr. Wacko."

I stood up. "No. Please, no pranks."

"Miss Kelly can't do it," Soup said. "She's too busy teaching school. So I'd guess that Miss Boland would be quite grateful if somebody, aptly gifted, volunteers."

"Don't look at *me*," I said quickly.

"Who'd look at you, old tiger? You're hardly in a proper costume to play in a pageant. So, if you'll excuse a phrase, keep your pants on."

Before I could inquire about the pageant writing that Soup had in mind, he leaped onto the bench, waving his hands in the air. His face was awash with inspiration.

"Rob," he hooted. "It's gotta be *you!* No better way to impress Norma Jean than becoming a writer, an author. Why, I can see it all now. Your name on half the books in the library. She might forget that you smell of *cow*."

"Will you help me?" I asked Soup.

"Count on it," he said. "After involving you with Crazy Horse, I sort of owe you something. But remember, *you* are the future author. Robert Newton Peck is a natural author's name."

I already knew what Soup would grow up to be. An inmate! In a jail or an asylum. A number beneath his face.

"While I," Soup continued, "shall become a preacher. The Most Reverend Luther Wesley Vinson, better known as the first Protestant pope. *You*, good Robert, will star in this theatrical triumph. And perhaps it will be your name alone that our fair community will blame . . . excuse me, I meant honor."

"Say," said Mr. Wacko, "don't you youngsters have to be home, for chores?"

"Quite," said Soup. "Sir, both Rob and I thank you for your cider, hospitality, and your remarkable command of the past."

Before we left, Mr. Wacko retrieved my pants from Crazy Horse. Fully clothed, we were fixing to head for home. Soup smelling fresh. I reeking of mule saliva.

"She'll remember ya," said Mr. Wacko as we patted Crazy Horse and gave her the rest of my carrot. "My mule don't forget people who are kind. Or who *ain't*."

On the way to our respective farms, Soup

Vinson said little. Yet, I could tell, my buddy was in thought. This could hardly result in a favorable fashion. Compared to Soup, both Crazy Horse and Mr. Wacko were pillars of normal behavior.

"Whatever it is," I said, "I don't want to do it."

Turning to me, Soup's face was blank of expression, as though he couldn't begin to believe that he'd heard my disclaimer.

"Then it's true, Rob? You have absolutely no desire to become a hero to Norma Jean Bissell?"

There it was. Soup's traditional taunt, one that held out a carrot on a stick in front of a mule. But the mule wasn't Crazy Horse. It was I, Rob Peck.

"No, you don't," I said through clenched teeth. "Not this time. Don't even imagine for a second that I'll be lured into another one of your Soup . . . insanities. Get yourself a new patsy, pal. I'm bowing out of this caper. And out of trouble."

Soup's nose elevated an inch.

"Education," he said, "not to mention culture, is not akin to insanity. Pageantry is artistry. We owe it to our friend Mr. Wacko. He deserves the town's respect. But we can't have a pageant unless somebody rolls up his sleeves and writes one."

"You expect *me* to write history?" I asked Soup.

He stopped. "Not alone. I plan to give you guidance, my boy, pointing your pen toward promise. But modesty forbids my hogging the glory."

"Maybe," I said, "we ought to ask permission."

Soup shook his head. "*Never* ask permission to enjoy the rainbows of life. If you do, some dull and colorless adult will say *no, no, no*. But if I do write the pageant, giving you full credit, of course, the erotic eyes of Norma Jean Bissell will yield to you and signal *yes, yes, yes*. Will you do it . . . for Norma Jean?"

"Yes, yes, yes," I said.

But then I remembered. Soup couldn't write. Not even a grocery list. All he'd write would be a suicide note. Mine! The only story Soup had ever attempted was about a shoe . . . a young sneaker that became an outlaw.

Soup had called it *Billy the Ked*.

Chapter 4

It was Saturday.

Believe it, we knew the knack to get in places *free*. So, following our early morning farm chores, Soup and I trotted to town to visit the Learning Free Library in order to bone up about 1776. As Soup read, I scribbled.

"Rob," he giggled, "take a peek at this." He pushed a book over my notes and under my nose. I read what it said about guns.

1776 Musket Procedure

1. Dumpeth gunpowder into musket muzzle, addeth teaspoon of flint, a pinch of sulphur, saltpeter, shortening, and a spark. Shaketh well before using.
2. Prepareth to get thine face re-paved.
3. Aimeth thy musket at Wahooligan's scalp.
4. Pulleth trigger.
5. After loud BOOOM (and one heck of a

stink), convinceth wounded Wahooligan that he now enjoyeth civilization.

"As I recall," said Soup, "it was the Pilgrims who brought the first guns when they shipped in on the *Mayflower*. And also the first funny hats."

"Maybe," I told Soup, "we ought to learn a bit about the Pilgrims and the *Mayflower*." I paused to think. "Say, how do you suppose those people thought up the name of Pilgrim?"

"Miss Kelly sort of answered that one," Soup said. "She told us that ocean liners show movies. So my guess is that all the *Mayflower* had was one old John Wayne flick that they featured over and over every night. Wanting to be American, the passengers started walking like John Wayne and talking like John Wayne, and even calling each other Pilgrim."

"And then," I said, "the Pilgrims landed and taught the Indians how to plant corn?"

"Righto," said Soup. "And in return, an Indian showed the Pilgrims a lot of useful Indian lore. For example, like how to open a clam or maybe a bingo casino."

"Was that Squato?" I asked.

Soup nodded. "He explained the favorite local sport to the Pilgrims. It was called lacrosse, or sometimes just Squat Tag . . . which is played in an open field, but never nakedly over corn stubble."

Reading on, we discovered the name of the chief of the Wahooligan tribe: Sitting Duck. And also the name of his flirty and full-figured daughter, Wet Blanket . . . a high-voltage gal in a low-voltage tepee.

As I read, Soup wrote.

"Ah," he said, "at last we may have our pageant's opening scene, in which a Wahooligan first encounters a Pilgrim who is armed with a gun, a big-bell blunderbuss musket."

I looked at what Soup had written.

Sitting Duck: "Ugh. Is that a blunderbuss?"
Colonist: "This? Shucks no. It's just a little ol' slide trombone."
Sitting Duck: "How's it work?"
Colonist: "Easy. Just giveth me your daughter and peepeth into this little black hole."

"Maybe," I told Soup, "we could insert some religion."

"No problem," Soup said. "We've got the Reverend Cotton Mather who, I think, invented the cotton gin, which made gin from cotton. He was very popular! Gin, however, was only for Protestants. The Catholics didn't drink. Instead, they ate a lot of hot Mexican food and prayed for clean underwear. Blessed art thou, and blessed is thy Fruit of the Loom."

"Soup," I asked, "is this stuff you're telling me really true?"

He grinned. "Well," he said slowly, "perhaps I did exercise a modicum of the proverbial poetic license."

"Then why are you saying all of this to me?"

"Because," Soup patiently explained, "I'm starting to consider what Mr. Wacko told us the other day. You remember, Rob. It was about tampering or tinkering with the truth."

"I recall. He said . . . 'If it ain't broke, don't fix it.'"

Soup punched my shoulder, friendly-like.

"Right, old tiger," he said. "Mr. Wacko warned us about when *politicians* start correcting. Apparently they can't leave good enough alone. Some want to rewrite the Bible. And change geographical boundary lines to win elections. Or start adjusting the census. And worse, dishonoring the Confederate flag."

"Yes," I agreed, "he talked about that. Mr. Wacko said that truth was our shining sword; and with it, you and I would combat any political correcting that we have to face."

"You got it," Soup said.

"Soup," I said, "something's bothering me."

"Spew it out or it'll fester."

"Well, it's sort of about Mr. Wacko's name, which really isn't Insanity. Maybe it's unfair.

28

Perhaps that's a name his enemies tagged onto him, because his real name is Sanity."

Soup nodded.

"Rob," he said in one of his rarely serious moments, "just maybe Mr. Sanity Wacko is the only sane historian we have in the entire town of Learning. And, old tiger, you and I shall revive his name with our productive pens of pageantry."

"Even though I can't quite believe that I'm actual admitting this," I told Soup, "I'm sort of glad we're writing the pageant for the Fourth of July."

"Me too." But then Soup fired me a half smile. "However, old sport, I'm not really writing it at all."

"Who is?"

"You are."

"Me?"

"Of course. It's entirely *yours*. After all, what would Norma Jean Bissell think, were she to discover that I, Luther Wesley Vinson, happened to ghostwrite our play?" Soup held up a hand. "Don't answer. Norma Jean might suspect that I'd stirred my spoon into your broth . . . and therefore, she and the entire town might suspect *both* of us."

"She would?"

"Indeed."

"What'll we do?" I asked my pal.

"Simple," he said. "You and I, old warrior, toiling as a team, will wield our wits and wisdom to conjure up a pageant script that will impress not only the fair Norma Jean Bissell, but rather this entire august community."

"We're going to do all *that?*"

Closing his eyes, Soup Vinson modestly nodded. "Honest," he said. "Robert, you and I are building history, in our own inimitable fashion. Perhaps like Noah built his wooden ark and then invited all the animals aboard."

"All of them?" I asked.

Soup shrugged. "Well," he said, "all except those two termites." He paused for a smirk. "Or," he said, "we'll be like the ancient Egyptian engineers who gave their Pharaoh his Sphincter and Pyramids."

"Not to mention," I said, "how our Continental Congress prayed for divine guidance and then, seeing the light, voted themselves a pay raise."

"But," said Soup, "to return to our revered . . . no pun intended . . . Fourth of July in 1776. 'Twas then Mr. Thomas Jefferson scrawled our Declaration of Independence." Soup suddenly sprang to his feet. "Rob, I can see it now! Mr. Jefferson's hoping that the members of Congress would pen their John Hancocks to his declaration. And threatening that if some comedian actual signs *John Hancock* as a joke, he'll make him eat it."

Standing, I shook his hand.

"Soup," I said, "we are really going to produce a pageant script that's worthy of all Learning's heritage. And," I added, "one that'll honor Mr. Sanity Wacko."

"Check," said Soup. But then he abruptly frowned. "Yet," he added, "I can foresee a minor problem."

"What is it?"

"Here in Learning, one faction may be rooting for factuality, which might be insisting that the British redcoats win. The other side, believe it or not, will maintain that our New England patriots ought to be rightful victors at Disability's Disaster."

Sweat began to dampen my face.

Soup was right. He and I could be mired smack-dab in the middle of a town tussle. A no-win situation in a losing battle.

Without saying more, Soup climbed out of his chair to stretch himself prone on the library's long reading table. Then I did the same. But the table wasn't too soft. Wood seldom is. Yet, as Soup did push-ups, there I lay, hoping that inspiration would arrive, as a visitor.

Someone did come.

"*This,*" said Mrs. Beehive, our librarian, "is not a gymnasium, nor is it a flophouse." She sighed. "What are you two hellions into?"

"History," said Soup. "We are writing a pageant."

"For school," I added quickly.

Just in time, Miss Boland arrived to convince

Mrs. Beehive that, indeed, we were. However, the pained expression on our county nurse's face was anything but confident.

Miss Boland sighed.

"Boys," she confessed, "thanks to you, we'll have a pageant script, but perhaps without any Disability, as Sharpton Dullard isn't able to act in it."

"Why not?" asked Mrs. Beehive. "He's so big and brawny that he'd be just perfect for the leading role."

"Because," Miss Boland explained, "it sort of seems that his brother Leroy fell off a roof and somehow landed on Sharpton. A pity. Sharpton Dullard would have played the ideal Disability Learning. He weighs close to three hundred and has the I.Q. of a gumdrop. But that big lumberjack is still meaner than sin."

"Ask somebody else," I suggested to Miss Boland.

"Already have. Sharpton is their ringleader. Without him, a lot of the others won't participate." Miss Boland's eyes suddenly caught fire. "Ah!" She jumped up and down. "But there's one more chance. If I ask *him*, he'll surely come. But we'll have to do it soon and sudden."

"Do what?" we asked Miss Boland.

"I'll have to send for . . . Buttercup."

Chapter 5

"Here we are," said Soup.

It was Saturday afternoon. An hour ago, Miss Boland had ordered Soup and me to visit the Grange Hall, to observe a first rehearsal.

"The music will inspire you," Miss Boland said, "and perhaps give you boys a few ideas to juice up our 1776 pageant."

We were almost the last to arrive. More than two dozen of our local citizens were already there, brandishing their assorted weapons of musical demolition. The conductor was also present and presiding. He, we knew, was the high school band teacher.

"Welcome," said Mr. Spitvalve to his volunteering musicians, "to the first rehearsal of our newly founded Learning Colonial Marching Fife and Drum Corps."

He said *corpse*, as most of those assembled were

beyond being senior citizens. The youngest was Miss Elspeth Elsworth, a senility-challenged seventy-five.

"Soon," said Mr. Spitvalve, "we'll be parading to the village green on Battle Victory Day, a term that Miss Boland has created for our Fourth of July event."

"I won't sit or march next to a tuba," said Mr. Wiltspire, sticking out his tongue at Mr. Hicky's tuba. "And I've never trusted anyone who plays one."

"Then," said Mr. Spitvalve, "Mr. Hicky, you sit beside Miss Notbright."

"Never," chirped Miss Notbright. "A tuba gives my ukulele asthma."

Yielding to artistic temperament, eleven corps members began bickering and changed their positions. Miss Notbright hid behind a piano and slept.

Mr. Jubert snarled at his new neighbor. "I never heard of a goldurn autoharp being allowed to play in a fife and drum."

"My autoharp," said Mrs. Fillpot, "sounds ten times better than a banjo with *no strings*."

"I couldn't find 'em," Mr. Jubert explained. "Besides, on a banjo it's the fingering that counts. I'll memorize all the tunes without strings and add 'em later on."

"How come we got a bugler?" Miss Dimwatt

asked, pointing at old Edgar Cramp. "A bugle won't add a thing."

Mr. Cramp winked. "That's her way of flirting me."

Mr. Spitvalve said, "Mr. Cramp, I see you're wearing your Spanish-American War uniform. Please don't wear it when we parade."

"Oh, yes, I will! I'm a veteran, and mighty proud of it. I'll be wearing my soldier suit. Or I won't wear anything at all."

Several ladies screamed. One fainted.

"Let's do *Indian Love Call*," said Mr. Hicky, "even though I don't know it."

"Is that a bugle call?" asked Mr. Cramp.

The door opened.

"Here comes trouble," Soup said. "This woman's a goody-nuffer."

"Sorry I'm late," said Mrs. Piperust. "I'll be your vocalist." She was carrying a hymnbook. "As you know, I sing first soprano in a church choir."

"With *her* voice," Soup muttered, "it's probable first stiletto. She could put a sign in front of her house that says 'Ears Pierced.'"

"What's a goody-nuffer?" I asked Soup.

"Somebody," he explained, "who's infected with religion and thinks she wrote the Bible. You know that old song." Soup sang: "*Gimme that old-time religion. It's goody-nuffer me.*"

36

"I say we warm up with a number that everybody knows," said Mr. Jubert, "like *Roll Me Over in the Clover*."

"I insist," said Mrs. Piperust, "that we do only hymns. My favorite happens to be number three hundred nineteen."

"Please," said Mr. Spitvalve, "turn to page seven in your songbooks."

"I'm missing page seven. Somebody stole it," said Mr. Wiltspire. "And I'll bet it was a tuba player."

Mr. Dampknicker was cussing. "Drat! I can't seem to open my infernal trombone case. At home, I always keep it locked."

"Goody," cackled Mr. Hicky. "You never had much lip."

"And I don't want any of yours."

From back in the corner, little Miss Notbright woke up and was saying, "I'd like to play *Blue Hawaii*. It's perfect for a ukulele."

"Not for *yours*," grunted Mr. Jubert. "My banjo twangs better with *no strings* than your pesky uke does on three."

"Four," shrieked Miss Notbright. "But one just snapped. Or maybe it was my garter."

"Ah," said Mr. Dampknicker, "lucky I brung my key ring. But I'll have to try all twenty-nine. Can't recall which key opens it."

"Let's attempt a march," said Mr. Spitvalve. "Now then, if I may please have everyone's attention . . ."

"I vote for a waltz," voted Miss Dimwatt. "Because it's easier to march to."

"Make it in the key of G," said Mr. Hicky.

"Wrong key," said Mr. Dampknicker. "This little brass one unlocks my doghouse. Trouble is, my little dog, Puddles, up and disappeared. He's been gone close to twenty years."

"Only march I could ever play," confessed Miss Elsworth, "was *The Beer Barrel Polka.* Then, years later, someone told me it was a waltz."

"We're going to play a *march*," said Spitvalve, stamping his foot. "Because I'm the leader. And we're *not* playing what *you* want to play. We are going to play"—he stamped again—"what *I* want to play."

"You're not playing anything, Spitvalve," said Mr. Hicky. "All you do is wave that little itty-bitty stick. And I'll tell you what you can do with it. Where the sun don't shine."

"March!" screamed Mr. Spitvalve. "March, march, *march!*"

That was when Mrs. Piperust started to sing *Onward, Christian Soldiers,* high-stepping around the hall as she sang. Until Mr. Hicky tripped her. As she fell she mentioned God.

"Nope," said Mr. Dampknicker, still struggling with his unopened trombone case. "It ain't this one. This here key goes to the cabinet where I used to keep the dog food."

"I'm glad Puddles left ya," said Mr. Jubert. "The poor little critter had to listen to all your sour trombone playing. My guess is that Puddles committed suicide. I bet he wanted to escape and run in front of a truck."

"Oh yeah?" the trombonist retorted. "Well, at least my trombone had *strings* on it."

Mr. Hicky was laughing at Mr. Dampknicker and calling him terrible names. But he quieted down after Miss Elsworth bopped him with her ukulele. That was when the fight started. Somebody, I can't recall just who, said that he never liked hymn number 319, or anybody who tried to sing it.

Mr. Dampknicker dropped his key ring. As he bent over to fetch it, Mr. Cramp stepped on his hand. Possible on purpose. Raising his bugle, Mr. Cramp tooted *Boots and Saddles*, which Mrs. Piperust couldn't seem to march to.

She slugged him with her hymnal.

"Rob," said Soup, "I think Miss Boland was right. This rehearsal of the Learning Colonial Marching Fife and Drum Corps will give us some useful ideas for our battle scene."

"Soup," I said, "I've noticed something weird. In this entire room, there isn't even one fife or one drum."

Fists were flying. In the middle of it all, Mr. Amos Dampknicker was still kneeling at his black trombone case, trying key after key.

"Golly," he said, "this is the final one. If this key doesn't fit, I'll just have to run to my brother-in-law's house. He's a custodian. There's over a hundred keys on his ring. Trouble is, he can't remember what any of 'em fit into."

But not everyone was fighting. A few tried to sing. Others swore, which sounded sweeter. One or two of the musicians were flipping through their music books, searching for a familiar selection.

"Let's play *There'll Be a Hot Time in the Old Town Tonight*," suggested Miss Twitty as she sawed her cello.

"My dear," said Mrs. Fillpot, "I think *Battle Hymn of the Republic* might be more in keeping."

"Look," said Soup.

"Where?"

"Over yonder. Mr. Dampknicker is smiling and holding up a key. I think he found the right one."

We watched as the trepidant trombonist inserted his last hope into the lock. I was glad for him. Maybe a trombone was what our musical assembly needed.

"It fits!" hooted Mr. Dampknicker. "Yahoo!"

For some reason, all fighting and foul language screeched to a halt. The hall quieted. A stillness vacuumed the air. Everyone crowded around our expectant trombonist as he slipped the correct key into his case.

I heard a tiny click.

"It works!" hollered Mr. Dampknicker. "My case is about to open. Hold on to your hats, folks. Here she goes!"

Slowly, as two little hinges were creaking, the trombone case opened. We all edged in for a long-awaited glimpse of Sears, Roebuck and Co.'s bargain brass. The lid lifted. I was glad, for Mr. Dampknicker's sake, that his case wasn't empty.

There, colder than ice fish and stiffer than a trombonist's upper lip, lay Puddles.

Chapter 6

"Makes one wonder," said Soup.

"About what?" I asked him.

"I'm wondering who Buttercup is."

Leaving the Grange Hall, we turned a corner by the Hot-to-Trot Jalapeño Diner, whose motto was "Burns both ways, coming and going," and crossed a street to our village park.

"Ah," said Soup. "Our hero of 1776."

"Yup," I said, "that's his statue."

There, immortalized in native stone, stood the leader of our 1776 militia, misnamed Disability Learning. To me the pose seemed cowardly, as our gray granite hero was running and looking back over his shoulder as though fleeing from the enemy. Most of his name was hidden by overgrown vines and shrubbery.

Several citizens were present, looking up at Mr. Learning, yet trying to put him down. Others, we learned as we approached, were defending him.

"He retreated."

"No. He advanced."

"Yeah. Advanced to the rear."

"It's that infernal know-it-all Boland woman," a man said. "*She's* the one that started all this bickering."

"Well, I think the pageant's a splendid idea."

"No, it ain't."

"Is so."

"Know what I heard? Miss Boland can't get nobody to play Disability's part. Because his battle in 1776 was a disaster."

"Like heck. It was a victory."

"All I know is, when I try out for a part, I plan to be a British redcoat. And my cousin Gelbert plans to do likewise."

"I'll admit you've got a point, Lem. Don't make a doohinky of sense to git ourselfs all gussied out in a uniform and then act on the losing side."

The men wandered off, still arguing. Yet the majority seemed to be favoring the British.

"Trouble," said Soup.

"How so?" I nervously asked.

"Rob, it's still June. But our big Fourth of July battle is already being fought."

There was an empty park bench near the statue, so Soup and I seated ourselves.

"Miss Boland," said Soup, "could become a target of abuse."

43

"No," I disagreed. "Everybody likes her. Our nurse is our spark plug that lights up Learning year after year."

"Ah," said Soup. "But nobody likes to lose."

A pigeon paused to light on one of the three corners of Disability's granite tricorn hat. It let out a "coo" and something else. Then flew off.

"Here's the problem," said Soup. "Half of the local men will have to play the New England patriots, the *losers*. This means half of the families in town will be angry. See?"

I saw. "I see," I said.

"However," said Soup, "if we write our pageant script so that the colonials win, and the redcoats lose, the exact same problem exists. And other tempers may flare."

"What'll we do? Make it a draw? A tie?"

Soup grinned.

"Rob, old tiger," he said, leaping to his feet, not bothering to brush the pigeon manure from the seat of his pants, "I got the solution!"

"They all kill each other?"

"Wrong."

Soup began to dance. Now there was no holding him. Somewhere, in some mythical time zone between Insanity Wacko and Crazy Horse, there lived a Luther Wesley Vinson. There he was, happily prancing, the only resident of Planet Idiotica.

"It was there all along, Rob, old sport. Plain as

44

day. Yet we failed to find it. Just now, it bounded out of the bushes of bewilderment to bash my brain."

Sitting on the bench, probable in other pigeon doo, I watched the local lunatic. Arms raised in triumph, Soup spun around and around. Then, without a word, he started to climb. Up, up, until he sat on Disability Learning's retreating shoulders.

"It's so obvious!" he shrieked to the sky.

Although it was a sunny June afternoon (best of all, a Saturday), a chill began to creep along my flesh, crawling up my spine.

"I know, Rob. Now I know who *wins*."

Sheriff Blood, I guessed. He'd catch us doing whatever Soup Vinson would have us do, arrest us, and we'd go packing off to prison. Eyes closed, I imagined I'd soon be reading a headline in our weekly newspaper:

NUTS NABBED

A pair of public enemies, identified by the authorities as Luther Wesley Vinson and Robert Newton Peck, were arrested on July 4. Without the needless formality of a trial, the two thugs were convicted and sentenced to hang. The judge and jury were approvingly cheered by all respectable Learning citizens, including their parents.

"Hey," I hollered up to Soup, "what can you actual see from up there on Mr. Learning's shoulders?"

"Not so much," he said, "because of all the leafy trees." He looked behind him. "But I sure got a nifty close-up view of Big Mouth."

Everybody in town knew about Big Mouth, our giant Revolutionary War cannon. She was big, black, and mounted on four mammoth wheels. But, needless to say, the huge cannon wasn't pointed at Mr. Learning's statue. She was about fifty yards away, up a steep hill, her muzzle aimed in the opposite direction.

I was certain glad that Big Mouth was rarely fired . . . except, of course, on every Fourth of July.

Looking up again at Soup, I advised him not to try to fly from up there.

Standing up, he flapped his arms, lost balance, and then came sliding and slipping down the statue, through countless pigeon deposits, to safety. Soup was a mess . . . in more ways than one. Yet, there he stood, singing, his manured face smiling with some secret uncontainable joy. There was only one Luther Wesley Vinson. Our universe wasn't quite resilient enough to survive two. Mr. and Mrs. Vinson must be grateful that he wasn't twins.

"Rob," he said, walking toward me, "I know how our pageant script is going to end. In a grand finale."

"How?"

Ignoring my question, Soup said, "What's more, I also got it all figured as to the characters you and I will be."

"Tell me."

Soup grinned. "It's a surprise."

Leaping off the bench, I said, "No. None of your stupid surprises. Whatever it is, scratch me off the list."

"Don't you *get* it, Rob?"

"Nope. And I certain don't *want* it," I said. "So don't bother to waste your breath, or my time, explaining your idiotic idea. I'm not interested."

"Okay, I'll tell you."

"The whole thing?"

"Well, most of it . . . depending on your need-to-know evaluation. So let's start up Main Street for home."

As I turned, Soup stopped.

"Rob," he said, "those bushes are covering Mr. Learning's name. Lend me a quick hand. I'll stand back here for a complete view, while you click open your jackknife and trim off a few of those pesky vines."

"Okay."

Soup supervised as I trimmed.

"Take another six inches off that twisty tendril on top," Soup suggested. "Good work, buddy. Now people can identify Mr. Learning's name."

As I read it, my eyes widened. "Soup, come close and take a squint at this. You won't believe what you're about to see."

He came, looked, and flinched. "Well, I'll be dipped in sheep dip. Somebody chipped off three of the letters on his first name, because the D-I-S is gone."

I nodded. The base of the statue now read ABILITY LEARNING.

"Let's go home," I said.

We walked. Briskly. The only way to walk is to hustle whenever you're reeking of pigeon.

In front of State Theater, my pal stopped. "There they are," Soup said. "The movies! Rob, think of how many cowboy pictures we've seen inside this place."

"Countless."

"Right you be. Here, old tiger, lies our answer. The solution to our pageant problem. An outcome that may bring smiles to the entire town in July. Grins instead of grimaces."

"Soup, you mean in a 1776 New England pageant, you and I are going to be . . . *cowboys?*"

"Robert, I give you my word. A solemn promise. We aren't going to be cowboys. Nor will we be on horseback."

I breathed a breath of relief.

Yet I was still befuddled. As we continued to walk uproad toward home, I knew that Soup

49

Vinson was surviving a recent brainstorm. One, I feared, that I would fail to survive. Visions of Sheriff Dillon Blood, our local cop, glowered before my eyes. He, and jail.

"Cowboys?" I asked Soup again.

"No. Cowboy *movies!* They always end in such a predictable way. Think about it."

I thought.

"Soup, I give up. If we're going to complete a competent 1776 pageant script, it certain can't be a cowboy movie."

"You're correct, Rob. Right on target. I knew you'd figure it out. Congratulations, old top. Because what we're going to plan is the direct *opposite* of every single cowboy movie that you and I have ever popcorned through."

The opposite?

That's where I ought to go. In the opposite direction of wherever Soup was headed. Run, and escape, never to look back.

"Soup," I said, "I smell trouble. With every passing second, the strong scent of impending doom is nagging my nostrils." I paused to take a breath. "And another thing is bugging me. At the foot of Ability Learning's statue, how come I was the only guy cutting away the vines?"

"Because," said Soup, "it was poison ivy."

Chapter 7

Monday came. So did school.

Miss Kelly, preparing us for Battle Victory Day on the Fourth of July, peppered us with history until heck wouldn't hold it.

For much of the past weekend, our teacher told us, she and Miss Boland had worked on costumes for the pageant. Red for the British, blue for the New England patriots.

"To my dismay," Miss Kelly informed us, "Miss Boland cleverly borrowed about twenty red jackets from the Flamers, our local volunteer fire department. And some white football pants from the high school athletic director, Coach Beefjerky."

"What about the patriots?" Soup asked. "What are the colonists going to wear?"

Miss Kelly smiled. "Years ago, Miss Boland was the captain of a ladies' baseball team, the Fly Catchers. They wore buff-colored bloomers. A shade of light cream."

"I bet for Miss Boland," Soup whispered to my ear, "it was probable heavy cream."

"For the patriot jackets," said Miss Kelly, "we borrowed blue uniform coats from the American Legion Band, which is now no longer, as a result of public demand."

The class mumbled an approval.

"So," said our teacher, "we're all set, as far as the colonist military uniforms go. Blue and buff."

"What about hats?" asked Norma Jean Bissell in a voice so melodic that all my glands tinkled like a wind harp.

"That," she said, "could have been a problem. As you know, three-sided tricorns aren't worn today. So Miss Boland worked up the courage to ask Mr. Slosh Dubinsky, at the pool parlor, if he'd lend us some old triangles. You know. What the pool shooters rack their balls in. Once we had the triangles, the rest was easy."

"Soup," I whispered, "you have to credit Miss Boland. She sure works at a project to make it fly. She's a large lady, and there's a lot of her to like."

"Indeed," Soup agreed. "That's why my solution about cowboy movies will protect our beloved county nurse from public ridicule."

"Miss Boland is really okay," I said. "So's Miss Kelly."

Right then, just as I had hardly mentioned Miss

Boland's name, through the door she blew. A big smile graced her face.

"Tidings," shouted Miss Boland, "of great joy!"

Because of our county nurse, I often wondered why we ever bothered with a weekly newspaper. Miss Boland was, by herself, some sort of a human news report.

"He's coming!" Miss Boland shrieked, whirling around and around in circular celebration, as though she'd become a two-hundred-pound cloud of confetti.

"Who?" asked Miss Kelly.

"Buttercup."

Soup and I leaned forward an inch, both of us intent on knowing exact who Buttercup really was.

"He," said our nurse, "is my baby brother."

"Wonderful," said Miss Kelly. "He's been away from Learning for so long a time. Years ago, in our youth, we all had so much fun together."

"Those were the days," agreed Miss Boland. "He was the cutest little baby you ever saw. All pink and cuddly. Big blue eyes. And he smelled sweeter than a flower. I guess that's why my parents named him Buttercup."

"Yes," said Miss Kelly, "I remember Buttercup. What a nice, polite little boy he always was."

"He grew up," said Miss Boland. "Over the years, he sent me a few photographs. He really did grow. I guess that's why somebody nicknamed him something else."

"As I recall," Miss Kelly added, "your baby brother never seemed too overjoyed with being Buttercup Boland. Not when he actual had to play the part of a buttercup in the high school nature play. His face was surrounded by yellow petals."

Miss Boland sighed.

"That," she said, "was a sorry evening. He had to waltz across the stage, dressed as a giant yellow flower. But then Sharpton Dullard tripped him. My brother crashed into the pit and injured half of the orchestra."

"He truly made a hit," said Miss Kelly.

Miss Boland nodded. "Buttercup took a lot of kidding. Not all of it was friendly. Sharpton Dullard kept calling him Butt. My brother felt so humiliated that he left town. Yet I suppose he's long since forgiven Sharpton."

"Of course he has," said Miss Kelly.

"Maybe so," Soup whispered. "And maybe no."

"What do you mean?" I asked him.

"Even," said Soup, "if I was a big lumbering lumberjack like Sharpton Dullard, I doubt that I'd want to trip another big guy, one who's a buttercup, in yellow, and has to flit across a stage."

"What are you thinking?" I asked my pal.

"Thoughts."

"Such as."

"Rob, what we heard is going to prove useful for our pageant's big battle scene."

"Soup," I pleaded, "let it go. Our script can't afford to agitate alarm or reopen old wounds."

Soup nudged me. "You're right, Robert. Causing trouble on Battle Victory Day, even though it might serve to enliven our theatrics, would be crazier than Crazy Horse."

"Good," I said, wondering why, for some unknown reason, I wasn't feeling any sense of relief.

"Don't worry," Soup told me.

Worry? Me worry? I had no cause for concern. Or did I? Perhaps I'd been working too hard on our script. Our upcoming Battle Victory Day was bound to be a resounding success. Now what could possible go wrong?

"Nothing," I said aloud in fervent hope.

"Huh?" Soup asked.

"Oh, nothing," I answered him. "I sometimes blurt out a *nothing* when I'm thinking about *something*. That's all."

"Don't worry," Soup said again. "I have it all planned. In my mind, our pageant and its residual repercussions are entirely mapped out. You'll be proud, Rob, to see Robert Newton Peck on the finished script."

"Listen up," said Miss Boland. "I've posted a few sign-up sheets. One's outside the fire station, other in the courthouse. There's even a sheet on the bulletin board at the community center. People can sign their names in the redcoat column or the patriot column. It ought to even out."

"Let's hope so," said Miss Kelly.

"Being the Fourth of July and all," Miss Boland said, "it might happen that a majority of our local fellows will have an urge to be patriots. Maybe all."

"What will you do?" asked our teacher.

"No problem." Miss Boland grinned. "I'll just use my charm and convince a few of the so-called patriots to be good sports. For a day, they can be British redcoats and have every bit as much fun."

"And your baby brother," Miss Kelly said, "is willing to lead the way, so to speak, and play the part of Mr. Learning of 1776."

"Right."

"I'm grateful," Miss Kelly said, "that you're not having to ask your brother to portray a little yellow buttercup."

"My brother's very big, and stronger than an ox. I seriously doubt there's a soul in town who could muster up the courage to call him Buttercup."

"Buttercup Boland," I heard Soup say. "Now why is that name slightly familiar?"

"Best you don't say that to his face," I said.

"Not a chance. Nobody will. Learning's a friendly town, with friendly folks. So don't be absurd, Rob. No one will even consider teasing somebody who's returning to our village to help us celebrate 1776."

Miss Boland looked at Soup and me.

"Luther and Robert," she said. "I presume you lads went to the Grange Hall to hear the music."

"Yes, we did." Soup winced.

"Good," said Miss Boland. "You'll see, on Battle Victory Day, nothing will stir the hearts of our citizens better than a marching corps of fifes and drums."

As she spoke, my heart felt sorry for poor Mr. Spitvalve, considering the talent level of his so-called musicians.

School let out.

"Okay," I said, "home we go."

"Not quite yet."

"Why not?"

"Well," said Soup, "a certain name rings a bell in my brain. I've seen it somewhere in print. So perhaps we might uncover a tidbit of interest if we stop by Petty's Barbershop."

"What for?" I asked Soup.

"Reading material."

We stopped by. Mr. Petty supplied us with a shabby stack of outdated magazines. Most were about baseball. A few about racing cars. Plus a girlie-girlie publication (well worn) entitled *Bamboo Bimbo* that featured several destitute young damsels in a jungle who couldn't afford many clothes. Another was called *Plowboy*. Several pages were missing, perhaps due to the wide-eyed enthusiasm of devoted collectors.

To my surprise, Soup threw *Bamboo Bimbo* and *Plowboy* aside, as well as all of the others. Save one.

"Now this issue," said Soup, "is exactly what we want." He held up a copy of *Piledriver*.

"It's about wrestling," I observed.

"Right," said Soup, searching through the tattered pages. "And, if our luck *holds*, pardon my wrestling a pun, we might spot a photograph of the person we're looking for." He stopped flipping. "Ah, here he is. Baby brother Buttercup."

I looked where Soup was pointing. It was a wrestler for sure, a very large one. He appeared mean and powerful. Then I read a name beneath the picture.

Butt (the Buffalo) Boland.

Chapter 8

Soup and I were on our way home.

That's when we saw something, and somebody, we didn't like. Janice Riker, with her slingshot, was zinging pebbles at Mr. Wacko's mule.

"Look," I said, "she's trying to hit Crazy Horse. We ought to run over there and make her stop."

Soup yelled. "Janice!"

She turned to look our way.

"Hey," I hollered, "I bet you can't hit *us*."

"Bet I can," she snarled. Bending, she selected a stone, loaded her weapon, and pulled the rubber back.

"Rob," said Soup, "prepare to duck."

Janice fired as we ran. But something seemed strange. A stone, instead of a cherry bomb, struck an oak just above our heads. The tree shuddered. So did I. Because the stone made me realize that Janice Riker was saving her cherry bombs, for some evil reason.

"Soup," I said, "let's hightail it."

We ran.

Janice, I was presuming, disliked Soup and me a lot more than she did Crazy Horse. Glancing over my shoulder, I could see that Janice was chasing us. This, I clearly recalled, was hardly unusual. For years, Soup Vinson and I had scampered away from Janice. For us, it was a form of physical fitness. But to Janice, however, it was target practice.

A second rock zoomed over our heads, whistling through the June afternoon sunshine.

No doubt about it, Janice Riker, who had a personality like battery acid, was tougher than Soup and me put together. Stronger, and meaner, but not faster. Janice was built for fight. We, for flee. Never could she catch us. Skinny would ever outdistance chunky. But, I wondered, could Soup and I outrun a slingshot? Sure as certain, we didn't intend to tarry long enough to learn.

As we fled, Janice followed.

Soup and I didn't have to pause to pick up pebbles. Janice did. So, with every second, Soup and I managed to hustle beyond her range. And hide. We hid behind an old shed, close to where Mr. Wacko resided.

There we waited. Keeping quiet.

"Where are youse guys?" I heard Janice Riker yelling.

Minute by minute, her voice seemed to grow fainter, farther away. We were saved.

I heard a noise. The door of Mr. Wacko's shack opened, and out he came. I smiled. It was nice to know we had a friend.

"Mr. Wacko," I said.

Turning, he spotted Soup and me.

"Well," he said, "guess my mule and I owe you boys a favor." He nodded. "Thanks a lot."

"Did you happen to see what happened?" I asked.

"Sure did. There's a few folks who hold to the idea that pestering an animal is honest sport. Well, it ain't. It's so much nicer to see youngsters bring a carrot to Crazy Horse. Instead of cruelty."

"Mr. Wacko," said Soup, "Rob and I are writing the script for the Battle Victory Day pageant."

Our old friend seemed surprised.

"Good," he said.

"And," Soup added, "thanks to your advice, sir, we know what to do about having the New England patriots win the battle. In fact, our idea is going to make everybody happy." Soup swallowed. "More or less."

"What's the plan?" Mr. Wacko asked us, looking at me with his question.

"Cowboys," I said, with a shrug.

"Not exactly," Soup broke in. "Yet, as I have

explained to Rob, this pageant's outcome won't get everyone upset."

"I can't wait," Mr. Wacko told us. "I'm starting to perk up a sincere interest in what's going to be happening on the Fourth of July."

"First off," I said, "there's to be a fife and drum corps. All local talent. Mr. Spitvalve, who's a band teacher at the high school, is in charge."

Mr. Wacko grinned.

"I like music," he said.

And so do I, I was thinking. But whatever it was that Soup and I had heard at the Grange Hall, nobody could actual label it melody. Instead, the newly formed Learning Colonial Marching Fife and Drum Corps was going to sound less like music and more like manufacturing.

It made me wonder how Mr. Spitvalve would be able to maintain his reputation as a music teacher. So much, I began to realize, was riding on Battle Victory Day.

Life in our town, I now mused, was a learning experience.

However, all was not lost. Miss Boland's baby brother would be coming to town. Baby? I'd already seen the photograph in *Piledriver* magazine. There he was: Butt (the Buffalo) Boland. He of muscle and might.

Well, at least Miss Boland was happy. Buttercup

was coming home to Learning to play the part of Ability. A celebrity would certain serve to brighten everyone's spirit.

"Come on," said Mr. Wacko. "Let's wander out to the pasture and pay a call to my mule. She's a good ol' gal. And, I bet, she'll be willing to make friends with a pair of decent boys."

Soup winked at me.

This, I concluded, was a part of his plan. Although I didn't exactly know which part.

Out to the pasture we went. The three of us. Four, counting the mule. To my surprise, Crazy Horse didn't act up crazy, possible because Mr. Wacko was with us. He petted her. And then Soup and I did.

"See," said Mr. Wacko. "Now you're all friendly. She'll remember. Mules, as I see it, are a mite more brainy than a horse. She remembers your carrots. And she'll also remember that mean Riker kid."

"Mr. Wacko," Soup asked our friend, "how did you ever happen to come up with the name of Crazy Horse for a mule?"

The elderly hermit blinked at us. "Boys, you mean to tell me that you don't know who Crazy Horse was?"

We admitted not knowing.

"I'll tell ya. Chief Crazy Horse was a Sioux. Years ago, away out west, there was a very famous battle. It got fought near the Little Bighorn. That's a river where General George Armstrong Custer made his famous Last Stand, against the Indians."

"Did he win?" I asked.

Mr. Wacko shook his head. "Nope. He sure didn't. In fact, that was the sorrowful end of General Custer. He lost the battle against Chief Crazy Horse and Yellow Hand."

I felt sad.

Mr. Wacko looked even sadder.

But not Soup. I noticed a slow smile beginning to spread across his freckles. Soup's eyes seemed to twinkle like tinsel. That's when Mr. Wacko and I got a surprise. And even Crazy Horse flinched.

Soup was jumping up and down, delirious with joy.

"Yes," he told us. "It's Custer's Last Stand."

Mr. Wacko turned to me. "Robert," he asked me, "have you ever considered taking your friend to see a head doctor? Or maybe even a witch doctor?"

"No," I said. "He's beyond help."

"Rob," said Soup, "it all fits. Remember what I explained to you about the cowboy movies? Well, this is it, old top. We've got the secret ingredient for our pageant."

It made little sense to me. Chief Crazy Horse and General Custer? Not in 1776. Because the battle at the Little Bighorn took place somewhere out west. Hundreds and hundreds of miles away. Nothing that Soup Vinson was saying, or implying, made a lick of sense.

"Mr. Wacko," said my pal, "I'm going to ask you a favor."

"Okay," said Mr. Wacko, "name it."

"Rob and I would like to borrow your old mule to play a part in our pageant. It's really important. So please give us your consent."

"You want to borrow Crazy Horse?"

Soup nodded. "Please."

"What for?"

Soup explained. "She'll play a pivotal role in Battle Victory Day. My friend Rob knows why."

"I do?" I asked Soup.

"You certain do, old tiger. Because, as you know, Buttercup is returning to town. Yet we can't allow his coming to turn into a disaster. Can we?"

"No," I said, "I reckon not."

"Ah," said Soup. "It's all set."

"Hold it," I told him. "Hold it right there. My mother warned me not to get myself involved in any more of your ridiculous *plans*. What's more, *your mother* said you weren't going to think up some horrible scheme to tilt us into trouble."

Soup didn't answer. Instead, he merely threw his arms around Crazy Horse's neck and hugged her.

"Luther," I said, "you're about to ruin everything. I just know it. My stomach is acting up. I hope you're not intending to have Buttercup dress up as Ability Learning and ride a mule."

"Don't call me Luther."

"I usual don't. But right now I can think of a lot of names, dirty ones, that I'm fixing to call you."

"Come on, Rob. Because we don't have a second to waste. We've got to get home, for chores."

We said a hurried "so long" to both Crazy Horse and Mr. Wacko, and turned uproad. With every step, however, I was wondering and worrying about what Soup Vinson had planned.

"Rob," said my pal as we continued toward our respective farms, "I got a hunch who knocked the D-I-S letters off Mr. Learning's statue, so it would say Ability instead of Disability."

"Who?"

Soup grinned at me. "Mr. Sanity Wacko."

Chapter 9

I was sleeping.

In my dream, I wasn't Rob Peck, but General George Armstrong Custer, wearing a blue coat and buff bloomers, on a horse. I was preparing for the Sioux to attack. Mr. Spitvalve was my bugler.

He called his bugle Little Bighorn.

"Where," I asked him, "is our fife and drum corps?"

"Still fighting," he told me. "They bash each other's heads so often that they're changing the name of our band to the Blunt Instruments."

He tooted Little Bighorn again.

"What are you bugling?" I asked him.

"Hymn 319."

Chief Crazy Horse appeared in white football pants and began to sing *Yankee Doodle*. Handing me his baseball glove, he said, "Here, I'll lend you a Yellow Hand."

Sitting Duck was there too.

"Before white man come, many buffalo. All eating buttercups," said Sitting Duck. Then he whooped a "wahoo."

"No," I corrected him, "it's Wahooligan."

"Sorry. Say, are you General Custer?"

"Not really. I'm Rob Peck."

"Rob," said Crazy Horse. "Rob Rob Rob Rob." But it wasn't *his* voice that kept repeating my name like a tom-tom drum. It was Soup's.

I opened my eyes.

"Rob," said Soup, outside my window. "Wake up, tiger."

Looking out into the blackness, I blinked, rubbed my eyes, and saw good old Luther Vinson below me.

"Hurry," he said. "We don't have too much time. Come on down and help."

I yawned. "It's the middle of the night. And be quiet," I whispered. "Or you'll wake up my folks."

"Are you coming? Norma Jean Bissell is waiting for you. Rob, you can't disappoint Norma Jean. I've got it figured how you can stop smelling like a cow."

Whenever I'm half asleep, I'll believe anything. Maybe I was still sleeping, and this was merely Act II of my dream. So, yanking on my pants (the ones with a rip in the seat), I sneaked out my window. Inching down our slanted woodshed roof, I stopped at the maple tree, grabbed a branch, and jumped swinging to the ground. My pants fell down.

Soup was there.

"Is this a dream?" I asked him, feeling my eyelids slowly sink to half-mast.

"Of course," Soup answered with a sly smile. "That's why you're moving so slowly. If you don't believe me, prove it to yourself. Before pulling your pants up, try to run. Nobody runs in a dream."

Eyes halfway open, I attempted to trot a few paces. But my pants were wadded around my ankles, so I barely budged.

"Good," I agreed. "I'm still asleep."

"Okay. Yank up your pants and let's go."

"Where?" I asked.

"We have to visit The Dump," said Soup as we walked. He pulled a paper from his pocket and unfolded it. "This is a blueprint. Part of my strategy, one might say."

"What sort of strategy?"

"Military."

The Dump was dark. Yet, because Soup had dragged me here so many times, The Dump almost seemed like home. Every pile of trash looked familiar. Especially under moonlight.

"Is Norma Jean here?" I asked Soup.

He grinned. "Yes. That's right. And your mission, old top, is to start looking." Soup paused. "And by the way, while you're searching to find her, find us some eggbeaters. Each with a handle and a crank."

"We didn't bring any eggs," I said.

"In that case," Soup said, "a broken eggbeater will suffice. So look around. Find two."

"Why do we need two eggbeaters?"

"So there's one for each of us."

While I was stirring through one pile of junk, Soup pawed into another. I heard him hum as he hunted, happier than a hog in heaven. For some odd reason, to Soup, trash was treasure.

"Eureka!" he chirped. "I found one."

"An eggbeater?"

"No. A big overstuffed chair. Rob, where there's a chair like so, there's gotta be an overstuffed cushion. Behold! Here it is. And we lucked out, old sport."

"Why?"

"Because it's torn in the center. That'll make it lots easier to pull out some stuffing."

As Soup furiously extracted and discarded, several handfuls of stuff were tossed toward the stars.

"What's that old seat for?"

"A seat of Learning," said Soup. "For two."

"Soup," I said, after a few minutes of searching, "I found an old eggbeater." I held it up. "Here it is."

"Good. Find another. Because I just stumbled across a little exercise dumbbell. Now all we need is a blanket, a few large curtain rings, and plenty of belts."

"Belts?"

"Yes. If they have buckles on them, Rob, so much the better. Green belts would be nice. Because our cushion seems to be green."

"So's my stomach. This place stinks like the whole world is rotten."

Soup stopped.

"Robert, old top, my world has never been rotten. It's been rich. Look at us right now. Here we are among prizes. Too numerous to count. Like we actual own an entire general store. And all this merchandise is *free*."

"You can have it," I told Soup.

"I'll take it," he said, bouncing on a mound of old chair cushions, arms in the air. "If I could, Rob, I'd drag it all home. That's my dream, partner."

"What's your dream?"

"To transfer The Dump to my own backyard. So, whenever I need a supply of something, there it all is." He kept springing up and down. "Wouldn't that be great? Then I could put up a big sign: MINE." He stopped jumping. "Sorry, old bean. Guess I got carried away."

Someday, I was dreading, men in white coats would come to the Vinsons' house and carry away Insanity Luther. To a cage. It was only a matter of time. Learning couldn't keep on allowing him to run around loose. My pal ought to become the main attraction at a zoo. Still and all, I had to admit that Soup Vinson was a likable lunatic. So, with a sigh, I continued to search for another egg-beater. For what kind of a contraption I had no clue.

"What are you looking for, Rob?"

I told him.

"Stout chap," Soup said, clapping a hand to my weary shoulder. "That's what Vermont needs. A dozen more stout hearts like you."

As I stumbled and tumbled and fumbled through the endless debris, I realized that Soup had no intention of telling me why we were here, in The Dump, at midnight. But by now, of course, midnight had probable come and gone.

"Hey," said Soup, "here's a belt."

Smelling all the trash, I smelled trouble.

"Trouble is," Soup admitted, "every time I find something here that's a real winner and drag it home, my mother always makes me tug it back."

"Speaking of home," I said to another box of junk, "perhaps we ought to go there."

I found some belts. So did Soup. Then he also located a moth-eaten blanket.

"Right," said Soup, "but first we'd better think of a secret hiding place for this stuff. It's too valu-able to leave lying around in the open. Some nut might come along and steal it."

"Only a nut would want it," I told Soup.

"Who'd want a dumbbell, one half-empty chair cushion, a collection of old belts, some worthless blanket, plus an eggbeater?"

"Yippee," said Soup.

"Now what?"

"Speaking of eggbeaters," Soup said, "I found us another. Two will be enough."

"Are you certain? I'd hate to leave this scenic spot knowing that we only had two eggbeaters."

"Here," said Soup. "Here's an empty crate. Well, sort of empty, except for a dead rat. But it's the perfect treasure chest to contain our loot."

Soup and I loaded our findings into the crate, marked it with a pole, and headed for home.

We made it to my house. However, because the moon had ducked behind some clouds, the night was pitch black. Not even a single star. So Soup and I did what we'd always done late at night. I walked halfway to his house. We shook hands. Then we turned and raced for our own homes, through darkness.

I hoped Soup was as scared as I was.

Chapter 10

"Hey! He's here," said Soup.

On the day following our night at The Dump, the two of us were in town, after school. That's when we saw him.

Butt (the Buffalo) Boland.

He'd come to Learning on a motorcycle. A large one. The hungry Harley-Davidson roared once, louder than Africa on fire, and then silently fumed to rest. Buttercup Boland's machine pointed directly at Soup and me. Butt's boots touched ground on both sides. He was dressed entirely in black.

To me, Butt seemed to be alone on his motorcycle. A second later, however, I realized I'd been mistaken.

Buttercup had brought a passenger.

A *girl*.

Miss Boland spotted her baby brother almost at the same moment. Forward she ran. He stood, and the two large Bolands hugged each other.

Soup and I approached with a caution that was rapidly yielding to curiosity. The closer we came, the bigger Butt appeared to be. It was hard to believe that all of him was only one person. To me, he looked more like a crowd.

"Brother," said our nurse, "welcome home!"

"Gee, thanks, Sis. I'd be pleasured if you'd meet my latest patootsie. Here she be. The object of my affliction. Sis, allow me to present . . . Miss Freebee Cookysheet." Turning to his beloved, Butt added, "Free, meet my big sister."

"No wonder we couldn't see her at first," I said. "Freebee's as tiny as a trinket."

Soup agreed. "I bet whenever it rains," he said, "she could hide under a mushroom."

Miss Boland smiled at Freebee. "I hope my baby brother treats you like a gentleman."

Freebee nodded. "Yes, indeed, he does. Why, there ain't a man in the whole wide world sweeter than my Buttercup."

Butt and Freebee were holding hands.

Soup, observing the pair of lovebirds, added his blessing by making a disgusting noise. "The bigger the wrestler," he said, "the harder he falls." Soup was frowning. Yet only for a moment. His face suddenly warmed to an impish grin. This, I knew, meant that my pal's brain was ticking. Much, I feared, like a time bomb. "Rob," he said softly, "our pageant's plot begins to thicken."

Into, I guessed, nothing but quicksand.

"Before the sun sets on this day," Soup announced, "our script will be ready. And willing. I got me a hunch that our Battle Victory Day pageant in honor of 1776 will require very little acting. Instead, we aim our musketry at realism. The stark variety."

"What does all that mean?"

"Our histrionics will have our hams being far more hysterical than historical. Let's go write."

Again we visited the Learning Free Library. While I researched more facts about Disability's Disaster (as it was unkindly called), my pal ignored my suggestions and wrote another scene.

"Rob," he said, "now I final realize what had previously been missing in our 1776 script."

"I give up. Give out."

Soup grinned. "Romance. One time I overheard Miss Boland telling Miss Kelly that every successful historical novel is spicy."

"You mean it has horseradish," I said.

"Not quite. I mean zesty, tangy, peppery, nippy, and burning hot. That, my lad, is the spice we're adding."

"Two people in love?"

To my surprise, Soup shook his head. "Two might be dramatically dull. But *three?* Ah, there we grab it. A beautiful maiden and two desirous gentlemen."

"Who are they? I haven't found any lovers in *Hotbeds of History*. And there's nothing on the subject here in the library. Not in all this dry stuff."

"We're adding moisturizer," said Soup.

"How?"

"Pig simple. While you were admiring Butt's motorcycle, I was noticing Miss Freebee. Yet I wasn't the only guy in Learning who was eyeing her. Somebody else was also assessing her, from the rear. Appreciating her engineering."

"Who?" I asked.

"Sharpton Dullard."

"He was? But Freebee is Butt's . . . Butt's . . . what was that word he used to describe her?"

"Patootsie."

"That's the word," I said.

Soup laughed. "Two may be company, but three is a triangle. And the triangle I'm cooking up will prove far more entertaining than any pool table rack inside a tricorn hat."

I nodded.

"Buttercup Boland," said Soup, "has come to play Ability Learning, leader of our local patriots. So you can count on Sharpton Dullard to sign up on the opposing army, the British redcoats." Soup chuckled. "Our battle scene is almost writing itself."

"How do you mean?" I asked Soup.

"Miss Boland will accept our casting suggestions.

And we shall suggest that Sharpton plays the British commander."

"Colonel Doughboy-Pillsbury?"

"Exactly," said Soup. "We'll convince Mr. Wacko to be Sitting Duck. The clincher, however, is the lady who plays his shapely daughter."

"Wet Blanket," I said. "Is that why we needed a blanket last night when we sneaked over to The Dump?"

Soup sighed. "Rob, listen to me. How would you feel if Eddy Tacker started to moon-dog Norma Jean Bissell?"

My puny fists doubled. "Angry," I said. "I'd be raging mad and ready to do battle." I gulped. "Even against Eddy."

Soup smiled. "Wet Blanket," he said, "will be played by Miss Freebee Cookysheet. She's the prize. A bone between two dogs. Or better yet, a dog between two boneheads."

I scratched my head.

"Soup," I said, "I'm still wondering about all that stuff we collected at The Dump. None of it seems to fit into our pageant. It's out somewhere in left field. Like a cowboy movie."

"Don't bother me. I'm writing your script. Rob, just think. Some future day, a fan will ask you how you got started as a writer. Here, before us, is your answer. You'll be able to tell people that your

80

writing career all began on Battle Victory Day, in Learning."

"I've got another question, Soup."

"Okay, what is it?"

"How do you know that Freebee will agree to play Wet Blanket?" I asked. "Maybe she can't act."

"Of course she can't act! This is show business. As it so happens, Miss Freebee Cookysheet is somebody's patootsie. In Hollywood, that's how stars are born."

"Hey," I said to Soup, "how do *you* happen to know all this stuff?"

"Simple," Soup said, grinning. "Our family dentist, Dr. Drilljoy, just happens to be a perennial subscriber to *Filmland Frolics.* And several outdated issues always seem to grace the magazine table in his waiting room."

Soup continued to write, and words seemed to be exploding from his pencil, intent on destroying the paper. And me. As he wrote, I glanced down at the front cover of his script. There it was, precisely as I feared, printed there for everybody in town to see:

Battle Victory Day
A 1776 study of how a writer takes liberties
. . . or death.
by Robert Newton Peck

"Don't worry," Soup told me.

"I'm worrying. Freebee, once she's aware of all this, can't possibly agree to play Wet Blanket. Because she'll refuse to be a bone between two dogs: Sharpton and Butt."

"Wrong," said Soup. "She'll leap at the chance. Freebee is itching to become, for lack of a more aspiring title, Mrs. Butt. So, we put a bug in Miss Boland's ear. And then Freebee, who's absolutely breathless to impress all of the Boland family, will cooperate."

I groaned.

"Okay, but I still don't quite understand all that junk we collected at The Dump. What are we going to do between two eggbeaters?"

Soup smiled. "As a dramatist might paraphrase, you can't make a *Hamlet* without breaking a few legs."

Chapter 11

Miss Boland seemed, to use a theatrical term, downcast.

"Luther and Robert," she confided in us, "a slight problem has suddenly surfaced. All of our sign-up sheets are rather out of kilter."

"What's wrong?" I asked her.

"Well, for starters," Miss Boland said, "it seems that all . . . I do mean *all* . . . of our local gentlemen are volunteering to be British redcoats." She made a wry face. "And I'm starting to figure out just why."

"Why?" Soup asked.

"Sharpton Dullard. That big lumberjack is sort of a ringleader here in town. And I'm uncertain that Sharpton is overjoyed that my baby brother, Buttercup, has final come home and is receiving a warm welcome."

"Who's signed up for redcoats?" Soup asked.

Fishing into her pocketbook, our county nurse extracted a piece of paper. It was a list of all the local roughnecks who'd signed up to be British redcoats. So they could be the official winners at what earlier had been termed as Disability's Disaster.

"Here they are." Miss Boland showed us. "And every one of them is a lumberjack, like big Sharpton."

REDCOATS

Sharpton Dullard
Flab Fuller
Leroy Deadbolt
Paunchy Sawicky
Lard Larsen
Braindead Dooley
Glob Smith

"These," said Miss Boland, "plus, I would guess, a regiment of other rotund rowdies. So, last evening, I asked Buttercup to make a telephone call and invite a few of his associates. I presume they're all wrestlers with lots of in-the-ring acting experience."

"When are Buttercup's friends coming?" I asked Miss Boland.

"Today," she told us. "My brother said they might be arriving on a bus. And I sure do hope they get here in time to try on their New England patriot uniforms. They'll look cute in buff bloomers."

"The script's completed," Soup informed our nurse. "Rob wrote near about the entire thing."

Miss Boland patted my head. "Thank you, Robert. As you know, history was never one of my strong points. I'm not a writer. Besides that, I've got so many other details that beg tending."

"There's a part for you in the pageant," Soup said to Miss Boland.

"For *me*? I'm not an actress."

"You won't have to be," said Soup. "It's not a talking role. So you won't be suffering from stage fright. All you do is stand there, Miss Boland, wearing your Wahooligan costume."

Wide-eyed, I looked at Soup. This was news to me, because he hadn't mentioned that Miss Boland would be playing a part.

"Goody," said Miss Boland. "As you know, I love to gussy up as a character. So I'll prepare my Indian costume, and jolly quick."

"Good," said Soup.

"By the way," Miss Boland asked him, "now that I'm going to act as a Wahooligan, whom do I play?"

Soup grinned. "You," he said, "are Sitting Duck's squaw. He'll be your chief interest."

"Do I have a name?"

"Yes."

"Well, what character do I play?"

"Bold Beaver."

Miss Boland smiled. "Wonderful," she said, pointing to her mouth, "because I have two large front teeth."

No doubt Soup had noticed.

"You're also a mother," Soup said. "Because you and Chief Sitting Duck are the proud parents of a voluptuous daughter."

"Who might she be?"

"Wet Blanket," said Soup. "Rob and I have given the casting of characters a great deal of thought. We've decided who ought to play Wet Blanket."

"Who?"

"Your brother's girlfriend."

"Freebee?"

Soup nodded.

"Excellent idea, Luther. I'll ask her to do it." Miss Boland winced. "But what if she turns me down?"

Soup raised a restraining hand. "Miss Boland, maybe Buttercup ought to ask. If he did, I'm guessing that Miss Freebee would enthusiastically accept."

"Good thought. Luther Vinson, you certainly think of everything."

Soup winked. "Yes," he said modestly. "I try."

Hearing a loud and unexpected honk, I turned to the source of the noise. So did everyone else in town. Wow! What a bus. Instead of yellow, like a school bus, it was black all over. Yet a few dainty buttercups had been crudely painted here and there, as trim.

BOOM.

The big black bus backfired. Then stopped.

Its brakes hissed like a cornered cobra. As its door opened, the passengers stepped out. In my mind, there was absolutely no doubt who they all were. Each, in size, was similar to Butt. Or bigger. Butt (the Buffalo) Boland suddenly appeared, stepped forward, and greeted them. And what a joyous reunion it was, as the wrestlers pounded one another. Then they seemed to settle down, laughing happily and bragging about their broken bones.

Saying little, Soup pulled our ragged copy of *Piledriver* from his pants pocket. As we flipped through the worn pages of the wrestling magazine, Soup and I managed to identify several of our new arrivals. Butt we knew. And we gradually attached names to the rest of the mashed faces.

"The one in the blue shirt," said Soup, "with no sleeves. I think he's Thug Thompson. See the skull tattoo on his face?"

"Yep," I agreed, "that's old Thug."

Soup pointed. "The guy standing next to Sewerpipe Shea, biting the cap off a bottle. That's gotta be Fisty Fistula."

"Sure is. Behind him, the one with the bloody jacket. His name is Hogpile Hogan. And he's chewing up the bottle."

"The guy he just spit glass at," Soup said, "looks like he just might be Lugwrench the Luger."

"Right," I agreed. "But the guy that Lug just kneed is Jackhammer Jacoby. And to his right is Uppercut Upson, the one standing on Crusher Cauliflower's ear."

"No," Soup said, "that's L. Lambo Lambaste. But I can't seem to remember what the L stands for."

"Leper," I said.

The bus disgorged all passengers as though it were seasick. The wrestlers busily pulled mirrors and combs from their pockets in order to perfect their hair and cosmetics. A few adjusted their earrings.

"Isn't it peachy," said our county nurse, greeting them. "You're all here. Battle Victory Day is bound to be a happy happening."

"Maybe," said Soup to me, "and maybe not."

"What makes you say that?" I asked him.

"Observe," he said.

I looked. But, at the particular moment, Butt wasn't looking at what was going on behind his broad back. Sharpton Dullard had appeared on the scene. In the crowd, he was edging closer to where Miss Freebee Cookysheet was standing. Very close. So near that he could (and did) lean closer to whisper something in her ear.

"Soup," I said, "see what Sharpton's doing now. He's handing Freebee a flower."

A little yellow buttercup.

Chapter 12

Miss Kelly faced us all.

"Today," she said, "marks our final day of school."

Needless to say, we cheered.

Our teacher, eyeing the little bottle of Anacin on her desk, said, "*Everyone* in this room may look forward to a peaceful summer vacation."

Mumbles of approval swept through the room.

"In only a few more days," Miss Kelly went on to say, "we will celebrate the Fourth of July. As you know, our town is performing a pageant, in honor of Battle Victory Day. If we all pitch in, we can reward our friend Miss Boland with an event she shall forever cherish."

As she spoke, I was deeply involved in cherishing Norma Jean Bissell. Ah, the cherry of her cheek. Yet I was plagued by the problems of pageantry. Life, for me, wouldn't be a cherry.

It would be a pit.

Beside me, on our bench, perched like an expectant vulture, sat Luther Wesley Vinson.

Soup, I feared, had planned something to involve me, not in Disability's Disaster, but in my own. Last night, I couldn't sleep. Tossing and turning in bed, I kept worrying about what we'd collected at the dump. A chair cushion, a variety of belts, plus curtain rings, a dumbbell, and a blanket. Not to mention two eggbeaters. Nothing, I concluded, could assemble from so absurd an assortment. Not by anyone sane. But my pal was crazier than Crazy Horse.

Again, I was gazing at Norma Jean when Soup poked an elbow into my ribs.

"Rob," he whispered, "you won't believe what a heroic role we'll be playing in our pageant. And a certain young lady is going to be delirious at the derring of your do."

"What is it?" I asked in wild anticipation.

"There's only five of us," Soup said. "Yet, in our very own unassuming way, we shall rescue the entire town from, if I may employ a sorry term, Disability's Disaster."

"Five of us?"

Soup nodded. "A big five. Now, as soon as Miss Kelly decides to parole us, you and I, old tiger, have a cheerful chore to perform."

"What is it?" I asked, hoping I'd never know.

Soup grinned. "It's arts and crafts."

My day dragged. Miss Kelly lectured us all on history, and we had to study more about 1776, in *Hotbeds of History* by Dr. P. H. Dee. For some reason, Miss Kelly kept repeating his name. Why? I couldn't begin to guess. Then, as I'd ignored all else, our teacher decided to spring her major announcement.

"I have important news," Miss Kelly said. "A person of renown is going to visit Learning on Battle Victory Day. Someone famous. His name is Dr. P. H. Dee, and he is a — "

"Wrestler," said Janice Riker.

Miss Kelly flinched. "No, he is a scholar. Dr. Dee is dedicated to supervising as many historical pageants as possible, at taxpayers' expense, to see that all amateur productions adhere to established data and are historically and politically correct."

"Trouble," hissed Soup.

I cringed.

"Rob, we've taken a few *liberties*, to use a Revolutionary term, in composing *your* script. This old Dr. P. H. Dee geezer might muddy our waters. We may have to take drastic action."

"Please," I begged. "Whatever you're thinking, do not think it."

Soup Vinson braced his spine. "Robert, my boy, there comes a moment in the life of every hero, a time to counterpunch correctness and allow the winners to win."

"Redcoats or patriots?"

Without answering, Soup slyly smiled.

School let out. We scholars, standing in line at the door, shook hands with Miss Kelly, thanking her for enduring one more year that had gouged another notch in her soul. At least it had nudged her twelve months closer to retirement and eternal rest.

"Home we go," I said.

"Later," said Soup. "First, we hightail it toward The Dump, there to put together our prize."

Minutes later, there we were, unloading all of the elements that we had assembled on the night when I was convinced I was still sleeping.

"Okay," said Soup. "Here's my blueprint."

Viewing our assortment of trash, I had no clue as to Soup's intention. Worse yet, I was reluctant to ask, as my fingers fondled one of our twin eggbeaters. I spun its little crank.

"Rob," said Soup, "begin by looping all of our belts together. Don't ask me how. Just do it."

I did it.

"The little dumbbell," Soup said, "belongs in front, like this, handle straight up. See? Now only one of its ends shows. You and I hold down the middle, behind it, on the cushion."

"Where do the belts go?"

"Underneath, to serve as straps. Insert a few of them into the curtain rings."

"Why?"

Soup stared at me. "Rob, please don't tell me that you don't savvy it. Not after you and I have sat through all those cowboy movies." Without further explanation, Soup finished securing the dumbbell at one of the short sides of the rectangular chair cushion. "There," he said. "That's our horn."

"You mean," I asked him, "like a Little Bighorn?"

"Sort of. Next we handle the belts. They'll meander around the cushion. I've never constructed one of these before, so suffer along with me, gallant soldier."

I suffered.

Nothing that my pal was saying, or doing, served even a smack of sense. Having no idea what we were making, or why we were making it, contributed to my concern.

"Soup," I said, "there's only one way to end all of this. You and I had better pack up and run away from home. As far as we can."

"Retreat?"

I nodded. "Yes, to escape jail."

Soup stood straighter. "Rob, a Wahooligan never retreats. A Wahooligan advances, dead ahead, to reap the rewards of realism in spite of the cowboy movies."

"I don't get it," I told Soup.

I didn't. Why, I kept wondering, did Soup

persist in all this crazy cowboy chatter? It had nothing to do with 1776. Was this palaver a part of his pathetic procedure? I moaned. Had I been alive, I'd have cried.

To darken the day even worse, Dr. P. H. Dee was due to arrive in Learning to observe our local disaster. And, I fretted, to report all tamperings with the truth to the police. Soup and I would be arrested. I'd hang. And, after that, Papa and Mama would scold me forever.

"Why?" I asked Soup, while studying the mess we seemed to be making. "Why do we have to be *inventors?*"

"To be famous," Soup said. "Maybe next year Miss Kelly will give us an exam. And I want you to be well informed. So, let's consider ourselves as the brothers who invented the airplane, Wilbur and Orville Redenbacher."

"Okay."

"Tie an eggbeater on your side of the cushion," Soup instructed, "while I attach the other one on mine. Each eggbeater has to hang blades up and handle down."

"Anything you say," I said, too weary to argue, yet wondering why we needed belts and eggbeaters on a chair. All this, plus the fact that the blanket smelled like a horse. A dead one.

"It looks perfect," Soup said.

"I hope this gizmo isn't for me. Is it?"

"Well, it's actual for both of us. You in front, and I in rear. Behind you." Soup giggled. "Behind the dumbbell."

"Soup, how come I always go first?"

"Because," he sighed, "you're a born leader. Now all we have to do is prepare the two costumes that you and I shall wear. That'll be easy because we won't be wearing much."

"We're going to be in a *costume?*"

"Of course," said Soup. "We're the stars. We upstage Chief Sitting Duck and Bold Beaver and Wet Blanket." He smirked. "One might say that we're the Last of the Wahooligans."

"Thank goodness. For a while, I was afraid you wanted us to be cowboys . . . on horseback."

"Wahooligans," said Soup, giving his eggbeater a testing tug, "never rode horses. Here," he pointed to our thing, "is what we shall ride astride."

"An old ripped chair cushion?"

"You're catching on. Rob, it's all working out in my mind. We arrive at the battle scene with a peace pipe. You and I restore order. Not only do we save the pageant, we heal the petty bickering. Without bloodshed."

"If we're a couple of Wahooligans," I asked Soup, "exactly who are we? What do we use for names?"

"Me . . . Spreadeagle. You . . . Lonely Skunk."

My teeth gritted. "You're saying that you get to play an eagle, and I have to be a *skunk?*"

Soup grinned. "As luck would have it."

"Darn you, Soup," I said, kicking the cushion. "I can't impress Norma Jean by riding a beat-up eggbeater and calling myself Lonely Skunk."

"This," said Soup, pointing at our constructed contraption, "is more than you think. We sit here, the dumbbell is our horn, and our feet hang down to stuff into the eggbeater handles for stirrups."

"It's a saddle? So we can ride a *horse?*"

"No," said Soup. "We ride a mule."

Chapter 13

Dr. P. H. Dee came to town.

Soup and I were on hand to witness his arrival. Contrary to our expectations, Dr. Dee wasn't a little man. He was quite bulky, bigger than any lumberjack or wrestler. Almost the size of Miss Boland.

"My," said Miss Boland, hurriedly primping her hair. "Dr. Dee is rather handsome. I can't wait to tell him that I'm Bold Beaver."

Dr. P. H. Dee had brought along a supply of his textbooks to peddle. And our county nurse rushed to purchase one, insisting that he autograph it. She showed her copy of *Hotbeds of History* to anyone who was interested.

Few were.

"History," Miss Boland gushed to Dr. Dee, "always has been my very favorite area of interest. We citizens of Learning pride ourselves on the major role that our founder, Mr. Disembody

Learning, played in 1776, during the Civil War."

"Thank you, Miss Boland," said Dr. Dee. "As a state official, my purpose in coming here, as you know, is to supervise your pageant. Like any academic, I ignore factual trivia in order to be politically correct. I intend to make certain that all scenes and characters are authentic, to depict what we insist ought to have happened."

"A student," said Miss Boland, "wrote the entire script."

Dr. P. H. Dee seemed surprised. "A child wrote your pageant?"

"Yes, with the assistance of our librarian, Mrs. Beehive, and using all of the factual material in your book, *Hotheads of Hysteria.*"

Dr. Dee politically corrected her. "As the day after tomorrow is the Fourth of July," he said, "I shall devote the rest of today at your Learning Free Library, with the script, to insure that all drama and dialogue parallel the corrected version. Word for word."

"Capital," said Miss Boland, fluttering her lashes and giving our distinguished scholar a shy smile. "If I can assist you in any way, Dr. Dee, I'll be close by your side."

"You may," he said, "officially escort me to your library. But first, I shall require a copy of your script."

"It's home," said Miss Boland. "However, as soon as I take you to our library, I'll drive to my house and then promptly bring it to you."

Turning, they walked away together.

"Trouble," said Soup. "Big time."

In one second, I was wet with sweat.

"Are we in it?" I asked Soup.

"Up," he said, "to our mastoids. Unless, of course, we can scamper to Miss Boland's house, arriving and leaving before she does."

We ran.

Sneaking in her kitchen window, Soup and I looked everywhere. No script. Where, I was asking myself, would our county nurse hide it?

"Thank goodness," Soup said.

"You found it?"

"No. I was just expressing my gratitude that my name is not on it."

"Soup, you dirty rat." Pointing at him, I said, "You'd better help me locate that script of *yours*, and fast."

"Okay." He grinned. "I'm your pal."

We looked everywhere with no success at all. Then I heard Miss Boland's old Hoover motorcar wheeze to a stop. A car door opened, then closed.

"What'll we do, Soup?"

"First," he said, "let's not panic. We exit as we came in, same window. Then we run around to her front door and knock."

"Why?" I asked.

"You'll see."

We exited, ran to the front door, and knocked. Miss Boland, who by now was inside her parlor, answered our knock. She greeted us warmly, as usual.

"Here we are," said Soup. "To help you in any way we can." He smiled. "And, if you'll permit, for Rob to make one small change in the script."

"A change?" Miss Boland asked, her eyebrows rising.

Soup nodded. "A very slight one. Nevertheless, Rob and I want the pageant to be absolutely accurate, to win Dr. P. H. Dee's approval. We think it's important that he love Learning, and also *love* everyone in it." Soup smiled slowly. "The change we plan to make is to enlarge the romantic role of Bold Beaver."

Miss Boland couldn't have agreed more. Opening her black medical kit, which had been sitting in plain sight in the exact center of her kitchen table, she pulled out the script and handed it to Soup.

"Here it is, Luther. Mark your change. Right now. But please do hurry, as I still have a hundred chores to do before tomorrow."

Soup grabbed the script. "Thank you, Miss Boland. We'll be back in no time."

She looked shocked. "You're not intending to

take it somewhere, are you? And, if so, where to?"

"To the Learning Free Library," said Soup. "Rob will look up the fact we require, and I'll zap in the change." He looked at her with freckled innocence. "Should we then bring it back here to your house? As you're so busy on other details, is there anything . . . anything at all . . . Rob and I can do to help?"

"Yes," said Miss Boland. "It's perfect. Because Dr. P. H. Dee will be there at the library. So make the change and present the script to him. He'll be the largest man you see. Tell him that Bold Beaver sends her boldest regards."

Soup grinned.

"Miss Boland," he said happily, "you surely have a way of being able to think of everything."

"Thank you, Miss Boland," I said. "A whole lot." And I was aching to add, "You'll never know how much." Yet I kept quiet.

Script in hand, we ran. Needless to say, we fled in the opposite direction of the Learning Free Library. Snatching the script out of Soup's fingers, I stuffed it into my shirt. Though I didn't yet know exactly where, *Battle Victory Day* by Robert Newton Peck was destined to disappear. For today, tomorrow, and forever.

We stopped running.

"Whew," I wheezed. "We're out of trouble."

"No," said Soup, "we're not."

"Why aren't we?" My stomach suddenly spun a cartwheel.

"Because," said Soup, "there's one more problem that we'd better solve. And jolly quick. Hear?"

"A little problem?" I asked.

"No, a big problem."

"How big?"

"Bigger," said Soup, "than Butt the Buffalo."

I stopped. "That's it, Soup. I've had it with all your problems and plans and pageants." With a hand under my chin, I said, "Up to here. I'm going to the police station, confess, and turn myself in. Sheriff Blood can lock me up forever. At least I'll be away from *you*."

Soup laughed. "You'll be famous, Rob. You'll be the first convict to escape to jail."

"You," I spat, "and your foolish follies. I feel dumber than a dumbbell on a mule saddle. I want out."

Soup put a hand on my shoulder. "Rob, old scout, you and I are pals. Buddies. I can't do without *you* for a sidekick."

"But it's my side that always gets kicked. Not to mention another sensitive area."

"Cheer up, tiger."

"Why?"

"Because," said Soup, "luckily I have a *whole new plan!*"

Hearing that comforting news, I fell to the ground, rolling around and around in the dirt, wishing I'd been born in Brazil. Or never born at all.

"There's only one simple solution," said Soup, pacing back and forth as I rolled in regretful remorse along Vermont's topsoil.

Maybe, I was thinking, Luther Wesley Vinson really did have a cure. Somehow, he had always done it before and managed to extract the two of us from total destruction. So, like a lunkhead, I asked Soup about his idea.

"What's your plan?"

"Big," he said. "We go big. Because, dear pal, *big* is the size of our latest, and most threatening, barrier."

"I know," I said weakly. "Bigger than Buttercup."

"Soldier up, Rob. The pair of us better slink together on this caper. Because it certain isn't a one-boy job. However, this hoodwink is our only hope. Unless we can pull it off, we'll be in the broth. And I'm talking tough trouble."

I stood. "Okay," I asked, "what'll we do, Soup?"

My pal looked very determined as he answered. "We kidnap Dr. P. H. Dee."

Chapter 14

"I don't want to do it, Soup."

We stood behind the Methodist church, among boxes marked OLD CLOTHES COLLECTION. Soup was helping to button me into a pink polka-dot dress.

"Instead of a woman," I asked Soup, "why can't I be a man?"

"You're too small. Besides," said Soup, "there aren't any male clothes in these boxes. You've seen a Sears, Roebuck catalog. Women's clothing starts on page one and goes to page six hundred. Clothes for men start on six-oh-one and go to six-oh-three."

"All right," I sighed. "If there's really no other possible way, I'll be a little old lady."

Soup handed me a pair of high-heel shoes. While I pulled on long stockings, he jammed a flowery bonnet on my head, a hat with ribbons. After tying a bow beneath my chin, he hooked eyeglasses over my ears. There was no glass in them. No lenses. Only the empty wire rims.

Using a back alley instead of Main Street, we hurried toward the Learning Free Library. As we arrived at the rear door, I said, "I don't favor doing this."

"Rob," said Soup, "you're a perfect little old lady. The important thing is . . . remember everything I coached you to say. So let's go over it again."

I rehearsed one more time, fluttering my high little-old-lady voice: "How do you do, Dr. Dee. My name is Miss Hortense Stumplicker, and I'm president of our Learning Historical Society."

"Good," said Soup. "Dr. Dee will greet you. Then you'll explain that Miss Boland gave *you* the pageant script, to give *him*."

"But I *lost* it," I said, right on cue.

"Right," said Soup. "And then you ask Dr. Dee if he'd please be so kind as to help you *find* it. The two of you leave the library," said Soup, "turn right, and I'll be waiting at the railroad freight yard to spring our clever trap."

"Suppose he asks me questions?"

"Answer the best you can. You're an aging person, and you're often very mixed up. This'll confuse Dr. Dee. If you're really stuck, holler the *one word* that all little elderly ladies love to yell."

"What's the word?"

"Bingo!"

The dress I was wearing had a few lice, so I was

itching like fury. Worse yet was trying to walk on high heels. My ankle turned. I stumbled.

"Dr. Dee will think I've been drinking," I said.

"Never mind. But he may wonder why you're taking him across all those railroad tracks. So tell him that this is where you possible dropped the script."

"In a freight yard?"

"Rob, it's our only choice. The only game in town. We agreed, at this late date, we wouldn't be able to locate an empty piano crate inside a moving van. Or coax him into it. So, it's hop a freight train . . . or nothing."

I nodded. "Soup, won't he ask me what I was doing there?"

"Anytime he starts poking you with questions, you know exactly how to avoid answering. Tell me what I prompted you to say."

Rounding the corner of the library building, I said, "I tell Dr. Dee that my dear departed mother, God rest her soul, had the maiden name of Dee, but then married my father, Dr. Inglenook Dee Stumplicker."

"If he gets overly curious, start asking *him* questions. Or mention his book, but don't get the title right. Keep Dr. Dee confounded and off guard. Rob, you gotta pull it off, or we'll both maybe go to jail."

"You and your plans."

The library had closed. Dr. P. H. Dee, however, stoically stood on the front steps, checking his pocket watch, then looking up the street and down, appearing to be displeased.

"Go," said Soup.

He thrust me forward to my fate.

"Dr. Dee?" I squawked in a shaky soprano.

He turned. I introduced myself. Dr. Dee's eyebrows raised as he eyed my Methodical Old Clothes Collection costume. I pointed down the street. He asked where Miss Boland was. With a shrug, I kept pointing. As we left for the railroad yard, he asked questions, a dozen per minute. I smiled, nodded, and mentioned every Dee in the Stumplicker family. He told me this was odd, as *his* was the only Dee family in Vermont. I explained that we were originally Dee Su Dong from Hong Kong.

His questions kept coming. Rapid fire.

Whenever I was stumped (or licked) for a reply, I turned my ankle, tripped, and fell down.

Jumping up, I yelled "Bingo!"

Dr. Dee asked why I was hollering "Bingo!" so I explained that I was practicing, in order to become a better player.

Following my eleventh tumble, Dr. Dee wanted to know whatever it was I'd been drinking, because he was starting to need some of it for himself. "A good stiff some-of-it" was his exact phrase.

Just as I fell for the twelfth time, my glasses

came off. Dr. Dee helped me to my feet, then retrieved my spectacles, commenting that there was no glass in the rims. He inquired why I wore them. I told him that my vision was perfect, but the glasses prevented my ears from receding.

Saying nothing, Dr. Dee bit his lip. His left eye began to twitch.

My shoe broke. When Dr. Dee asked why I seemed to be limping, I explained that one of my shoes had lost its heel. He suggested that I carry my shoes instead of wearing them, so I did. Until I happened to step on a sharp pebble, and without thinking, shouted a very bad word.

A real zinger!

I didn't really know what the word meant. Only that I'd heard Janice Riker use it. Janice, I told Dr. Dee, used that pastoral term every time she bent over to pluck up a dandelion and was kicked by a cow. As I recalled, Janice had been kicked more than a hundred times, I told him, which gradually was lessening her desire to pick dandelions.

Soup had instructed me to bring Dr. Dee to one particular railroad freight car. But I couldn't remember which one.

"It's a red one," Soup had said.

But as I looked, all of the cars were a rusty red. I counted between twenty and thirty.

"Ah," I said to Dr. P. H. Dee. "There it is."

"Which one?" he asked me.

I pointed. "That red one."

Dr. Dee seemed befuddled, a state of mind that Soup had earlier predicted. We stepped over a train track. I made it. But Dr. Dee tripped and fell. His accident prompted me to tell him that I was truly sorry about the dirty tar spots on his trousers, and even sorrier about the long jagged rip at the knee.

He said the same word I had used.

Perhaps it was a mistake on my part to ask Dr. Dee what the word *meant*. Yet I did. He told me that the word aptly described our town of Learning and all of its residents, and that he doubted that he'd ever be visiting again . . . unless he was dragged here by wild horses.

During the time when Dr. Dee was bending over to inspect his unfortunate trouser leg, I looked around. And spotted Soup. He stood in an open doorway of a *red* freight car, one that said BURLING-TON on the side. Soup was motioning to me.

"Here we go, Dr. Dee," I said. "That's the very car where I misplaced the script, or my name isn't . . . isn't . . . Miss Gladice Lickstumper."

Dr. Dee stared at me with acute suspicion.

"I thought you said Hortense."

I cackled. "That's me. Gladice Hortense Stumplicker, but I rarely use Gladice, except on Sunday."

We stopped at the boxcar's open sliding door.

"In here," I said, pointing inside the empty

freight car. "This is where I was. Sometimes, I tend to turn a mite forgetful. Didn't feed my cat for over a month. Starved, poor critter. Just like Puddles. He was a dog."

"You starved your dog as well?"

"No," I said. "Puddles belonged to a trombone player, Mr. Dampknicker, who couldn't find the right key. But it didn't matter, because he's not a custodian and doesn't have either a trombone or a dog." I laughed. "Open-and-shut case."

Dr. Dee nervously wiped his face.

"And," I told him, "Mr. Jubert picks a banjo with no strings on it. To learn a new song."

"This town," Dr. Dee wheezed, trembling as if he'd sudden caught a fever. "All of you Learning people ought to be locked up. In straitjackets."

I decided to change the subject in order to adhere to Soup's plan. "This is the freight car," I said. "But I'm too feeble to crawl up in there. You know, since my operation. I had a hemorrhoid transplant. But right up inside here," I said, pointing. "That's where the pageant script is. Somewhere in the dark."

"Why," asked Dr. Dee, "were you here? What was the president of the Learning Historical Society doing in a boxcar?"

I tittered. "Promise you won't tell?"

"Yes." He sighed impatiently. "I promise."

"Crap game. Only place in town where a few of us ladies can shoot dice. And I won enough money to buy my own motorcycle. I plan to be a stunt rider and jump over a bus. Then, if that works, I'll buy a bus that can hurdle a motorcycle."

TOOOOOOT.

A whistle blew. It came from down the tracks at the engine end of the freight train, as though the train were fixing to leave town. This, I knew, was Soup's plan. Dr. Dee would be lured, by me, into an empty boxcar. As he searched in the dark for my script, Soup would slide the door shut. Then, whenever the train pulled out, so would Dr. P. H. Dee. He'd be trapped, and traveling. Kidnapped.

But I was too chicken to go through with it.

So I confessed. Told him who I was. And all about Soup's pageant, based on his book, *Hotlips of History*. I mentioned Mr. Insanity Wacko (who was also Sitting Duck) and Bold Beaver and Wet Blanket, Spreadeagle and me . . . Lonely Skunk. I described our saddle for Crazy Horse. I named all of the wrestlers, including Butt (the Buffalo) Boland, whose real name was Buttercup.

I went into detail concerning our fife and drum corps, apologizing that it featured neither drum nor fife. And that they called themselves the Blunt Instruments because they couldn't play in sharps.

Dr. Dee looked totally unglued. "Miss

Stumplapper, or whatever your name is, or was . . . how soon does this evening freight train leave town?"

The whistle blew again. A warning.

"Now," I said.

Just as Soup sneaked out of the empty boxcar, *into it* leaped Dr. P. H. Dee. Then, as he was sliding the heavy steel door closed, he smiled at me, madly laughing. His eyes rolled wildly.

"Ha, ha, ha," he said. "I shall fool you all. Pan Handle Dee is escaping. I'll never catch whatever disease or mental disorder that you people have, and *you'll never catch me*."

As the train left, I knew we'd never try.

Chapter 15

Another bus came.

Needless to say, Soup and I made certain that both of us were in town as it arrived. We knew it was coming, as well as who would be aboard. Yet never, not in a zillion years, could we have ever imagined this particular bus's parade of passengers.

"Rob," said Soup, "she did it."

I nodded. "She sure did."

Indeed so.

Freebee Cookysheet, better known locally as the personal patootsie of Butt Boland, apparently had telephoned all of her girl friends, inviting them to Learning in order to see her perform as Wet Blanket.

While the bus unloaded, Soup said, "These young ladies, I'd guess, are the possible patootsies of the other wrestlers, Butt's buddies."

"Maybe they're lady wrestlers," I said.

"Or," said Soup, "a zoo in clothes."

Miss Cookysheet had also appeared at the town's only bus stop, to greet her friends. And, as it turned out, to introduce each and every lady to Soup and me.

Eyes widening, Soup and I managed to gulp a greeting to the girls, one by one, as they disembarked.

We met Pain Webber and Tailhook and Roadkill (and the twins . . . a tag team named House Wrecker and Home Wrecker). We then met Toolbox and Miracle Whip and Bodyslam and Innerspring and Milk Dud and Dragknuckle and Headmistress and Love Handle and Venus Flytrap and Dairy Queen and Jumpstart. Last, but not least, because she was by far the most chubby of all, we got to meet Eatie Gourmet.

Even though these ladies were the girlfriends of the wrestlers, Butt and his buddies didn't seem to be present. But the local lumberjacks were there. Every single one.

Sharpton Dullard and his crew were enthusiastically welcoming our latest arrivals with eager smiles. Some even brought candy and flowers and pink fur handcuffs. Oddly enough, the lumberjacks didn't seem to be afraid of the lady wrestlers.

But, to be honest, I was.

Soup, however, was wearing a smile that was

slowly spreading across his freckles. "Sometimes," he said, "a pageant has a way of writing itself."

As he spoke, I thought Soup meant that our pageant would somehow *right itself* and turn out okay. I found myself also smiling. Perhaps our Disability's Disaster wouldn't be so disastrous.

"It'll be great," said Soup. "An historical epic, perhaps elevating the name of Learning to the heroic level of Hannibal himself."

"Who is Hannibal?" I asked.

"Rob," said Soup, "in case we have to take a history exam someday, you really ought to memorize a few facts. Hannibal was the fellow who crossed Missouri on an elephant."

"Luther and Robert!"

Turning, I saw Miss Boland (soon to be Bold Beaver), and she appeared to be slightly upset over something.

We greeted her.

"Boys," she said, "you won't believe this, but try as I might, I can't seem to locate Dr. P. H. Dee."

Soup and I looked at each other, neither of us uttering even one word. Certainly not I. Memories of being Miss Hortense Stumplicker might haunt me forever.

"Maybe he left town," said Soup with one of his innocent shrugs.

"Left town?" Miss Boland arched her eyebrows.

"Impossible. Today's the third day of July. We're supposed to have a dress rehearsal for the pageant, and Dr. Dee was to supervise. I know he had plans to edit the battle scene."

Soup nodded.

"As may others," he said.

Miss Boland eyed the bus, the group of lady wrestlers, and the gang of lumberjacks.

"Ah," she said, "it's nice to see so many scholarly people coming to Learning to view our Battle Victory Day pageant tomorrow. And even nicer to notice that our local citizens are giving our tourists a warm reception."

As she spoke, I observed Sharpton Dullard attempting to give Miss Freebee Cookysheet a tender tickle. But not in the ribs.

"Where is Buttercup?" I asked Miss Boland.

"Oh, my baby brother and his associates decided to hold snarling practice. Buttercup promised me that, later on, he and all of the other wrestlers would be available to rehearse."

"Sometimes," said Soup, "a theatrical event ought to be spontaneous. Our pageant might suffer from too much practice."

Miss Boland looked surprised. "Too much? We haven't had even *one* rehearsal. I don't have a script. Dr. Dee has somehow gotten lost. And, worse, I believe he's taken our only script with him."

"Miss Boland," said Soup hurriedly, "if you're going to play Bold Beaver in the *dress rehearsal,* don't you think you ought to get yourself a Wahooligan *dress?* You can't be a very convincing squaw for Chief Sitting Duck in what you're now wearing, a white nurse's uniform."

Miss Boland snapped her fingers.

"Right," she said. "Are both of you preparing your Wahooligan costumes? As I recall, Luther, you are to play Spreadeagle; and, Robert, you're to be Lonely Skunk."

"Correct," said Spreadeagle.

Lonely Skunk forced a smile.

Perhaps, I was thinking, I'd consider telling Norma Jean Bissell that my Wahooligan part was Chief Noble Elk, or some other name of equal stature. Impressing her as Lonely Skunk might challenge my dramatic talents.

"By the way," Miss Boland told us, "I do have a bit of cheerful news."

"What is it?" I asked.

"Mr. Dampknicker final located his missing trombone. But only half of it. Just the bell, you know, where the music comes out. He can't seem to find the slide. So he's making the bell into a blunderbuss, a gun, for Buttercup to carry in the pageant."

"Jolly," said Soup.

"Oh," said Miss Boland. "One more thing.

Please, both of you, help old Mr. Wacko to get ready and be on time. I've been missing a husband all my life, but I don't intend to be a Beaver without a Duck."

We promised her.

Miss Boland's face stopped smiling, as though recalling something else. Something unpleasant.

"About that script . . ." she started to say.

"Good for you, Miss Boland," said Soup. "You think of *everything*. So Rob and I will look everywhere that Dr. Dee might have gone here in town. Believe me, if we find the script, we'll deliver it to you at once."

"We certain will," I added, knowing that I'd ripped it into small bits, burned it, then buried the ashes behind our barn, at a depth of six feet. Under manure.

"Or," said Soup, "Rob will merely write another. We have a few modest ideas for a dramatic finish."

"We do?" I asked Soup, as Miss Boland had left us and was out of earshot.

"Yes," said Soup. "It's the pageant's grand finale, when you get to impress Norma Jean."

"How do I do that?"

"At top speed," said Soup.

Chapter 16

Our big pageant day dawned.

It was July fourth, anticipated by some (and dreaded by others) as Battle Victory Day, or B.V.D.

Soup and I hurried to The Dump, took off almost all of our clothes, then rubbed our naked bodies against the oldest and most rusty car we could find. We became red enough to look almost fully dressed. After sticking a few chicken feathers into our rusty underwear, we were suddenly war-whooping Wahooligans.

Spreadeagle and Lonely Skunk.

In town we saw several men pouring a generous keg of black gunpowder into Big Mouth, our village's only relic. Local legend persisted in claiming that Big Mouth was the largest cannon ever cast in 1776. Others disagreed, insisting that she was the biggest cannon on planet Earth.

A year before, as I dimly recalled, Soup and I

had stood in this very location, to watch Big Mouth being fed. It seemed to me that this year's charge of gunpowder was more bountiful than last year's. Perhaps to create a more impressive explosion. The men who were now pouring powder into her, quite obviously, had earlier poured something else into themselves, to celebrate the Fourth of July.

The loaders were overloaded . . . and so was Big Mouth.

We, all members of the cast, assembled behind the high school, as Miss Boland, our devoted director, had requested.

Everyone showed up. Lumberjacks as British redcoats in red jackets and white football pants. Wrestlers as New England patriots in blue and buff. Plus us, the five Wahooligans. Miss Boland, wrapped in a white lace tablecloth trimmed with beads and bottle caps, made a passable Bold Beaver. Mr. Wacko was Sitting Duck, swaddled in a moth-eaten bathrobe three times too large. On the other hand, Wet Blanket wore a costume that she could carry in a change purse.

Together (the above three plus Soup and me) we paraded to the village square, near Big Mouth, where our pageant would be performed.

"Places," commanded Miss Boland, who customarily took charge of just about everything and everyone. Yet nobody knew what to do, where to stand, or what to say. "Ad lib," said our nurse.

"Except for the so-called battle scene. For that, a dignified silent pantomime might be appropriate. Because, as you recall, there actually wasn't a . . ."

We took positions.

Wet Blanket, in her modest (change that to *brief*) attire, seemed to attract the audience's attention. The wide-eyed husbandry of Learning churlishly applauded, until every narrow-eyed wife covered her husband's eyes. Very little covered Wet Blanket except for a wisp of wool here, a bead or two there.

She was quickly approached by Sharpton Dullard (as the British redcoat commandant, Colonel Doughboy-Pillsbury).

He winked. "Good morrow, my fair Spreadeagle."

"Hot Blanket," hissed Miss Boland.

Sharpton eyed Freebee up and down, and hooted, "She looks more like No Blanket to me."

"Hey," warned Butt the Buffalo, "this here little ol' gal, Miss Wet Freebee, belongs to me. She's my *patootsie*. Get it?"

"Oh yeah?"

"Yeah!"

Miss Boland was hair-trigger quick to intervene. "Now," she said, "it's time for our fifers and drummers to make their entrance and entrance us with their music."

"Here we come," said Mr. Spitvalve.

124

Toward the village square marched the Blunt Instruments. Needless to say, not all in step with their leader. A few pieces had been added: a bagpipe, a police siren, a bicycle pump, one washboard strummed with thimbles, a crank-it-up Victrola, and several silent dog whistles.

Knees high, Mr. Spitvalve turned a precise column-right.

Only three musicians righted the corner with him. The remaining twenty continued to parade straight ahead, noses buried in their little music books, until they all but disappeared, wading into Putt's Pond. Hymn 319, or whatever it was, gurgled to a bubbling silence.

"My pants are too tight," complained Hogpile Hogan. "I can't even bend over to pick up a used cigarette butt in these buff-colored bloomers."

Sharpton winked at Wet Blanket.

"I wish you was a patriot, honey," he whispered, "because you'd look even cuter in the buff."

Butt (the Buffalo) Boland roared something at Sharpton, but I couldn't quite understand all the words. One of them, however, I recognized as a favorite of Janice's.

Impulsively, I looked around for her. It was a lifelong habit. Because whenever Janice Riker was in sight, she was far less dangerous. Soup and I fervently believed in what we called Survival Rules One and Two and Three:

1. Always know where Janice is.
2. Know what direction she's going.
3. Run the other way.

Wet Blanket left her position between her parents, Chief Sitting Duck and Bold Beaver, to stroll hip-swingingly across the green to stand between Butt and Sharpton. All males applauded.

"Where band?" asked Bold Beaver, in her most fluent Wahooliganese.

Soup pointed. "Over there," he told her. "Coming up out of pond. Mr. Hicky now empty water out of tuba. He pour it on Miss Notbright."

"In a way," Miss Boland whispered to us, "I'm rather relieved that Dr. P. H. Dee isn't here to monitor our pageant."

"Oh," I said, "so am I."

The Blunt Instruments, most of them wet and splattered with mud, staggered to where everyone was waiting, near Big Mouth.

Miss Boland was suddenly smiling. She, no doubt, had coached her baby brother to deliver a few pageant lines. I saw her nod at him, prompting Buttercup into action. There stood our Disability, holding half of a trombone, but no slide.

"Hear ye," recited Butt in a tiny timid voice, "hear ye all. I am . . . my name is . . . I forgot."

"Disability Learning," whispered Bold Beaver.

"That's me," said Buttercup, fidgeting in his blue tunic and buff bloomers. "And I hereby command the New England patriots not to fire at them redcoats, until they see the whites of their football pants."

Butt appeared not to remember any more of his major soliloquy. So, raising the bell half of Mr. Dampknicker's trombone to his shoulder (like a blunderbuss), Butt blew into the small end of the tube. The noise he produced didn't sound at all like a musket. More like a gastrointestinal event.

The audience clapped in approval. Butt smiled. His years of acting in the wrestling ring were, at last, paying off. He smiled again, this time at Wet Blanket, his patootsie, who was fluttering her fake eyelashes at Sharpton. And another local lumberjack was blowing kisses at Miracle Whip, the lady friend of Thug and Lug.

"Do song," grunted Bold Beaver. "You know, song about territorial rights."

Watching, I had a hunch that Miss Boland had noticed that both Sharpton and Butt seemed to be molesting No Blanket. Nevertheless, they sang, yet continued to fondle the Chief's dim but delectable daughter, in her skimpy costume.

Redcoat (sings): "This land is my land."

Patriot (also sings): "No. No. It's my land."
Sitting Duck (grunts): "Well, if you two twits want *my* opinion . . . POO on immigration."

Everyone applauded. Because, in Vermont, immigration was just about as popular as maple blight.

Inspired by the song, Flab Fuller happened to lean closer and pinch a nearby lady wrestler, Gear Box, a gesture that seemed to induce a resentful response from her wrestler boyfriend, Fisty Fistula.

Harsh words were exchanged.

Fangs were bared.

Milk Dud slapped Lard Larsen, causing Sewerpipe to warn Lard not to repeat his gentlemanly gesture.

"Rob," said Soup, "now's the time."

"For what?" I asked him.

Soup smiled.

"Tension is mounting," he said. "And so are we."

Chapter 17

We sneaked away.

Soup, so he claimed, had it all worked out. The two of us were to upstage the redcoat lumberjacks as they fought the patriot wrestlers. We'd enter as heroic peacemakers.

Soup raced to The Dump for our saddle, I to get Crazy Horse.

Soup appeared, toting the sorry object. Belts and eggbeaters were dragging on the ground. Yet our master saddle-maker seemed not to care.

Crazy Horse eyed the three of us (Soup, me, the saddle) with questioning glances, yet our mule held quiet as we slapped the saddle to her back and belted it tight into our curtain rings. An upside-down eggbeater dangled down at both flanks.

"Stirrups," explained Soup. "Let's mount up, Rob. It's time to bring our Wahooligan peace pipe to the battle scene."

"We don't have a peace pipe."

"Ah," said Soup, "but we do. I think of every-thing. Stirrups or peace pipes or kidnapping. You name it . . . I think of it."

"Where's our peace pipe?"

"In my underwear," Soup said. "Early this morning I was wondering what a peace pipe would look like. It hit me! Merely like a *piece of pipe*. So, before my parents were up, I took a hacksaw and detached a short length of pipe from under Mom's kitchen sink. She'll never miss it. Unless she runs the water."

He showed me his prize. Instead of a pipe, it looked closer to being a dirty cigar.

"It's not long," said Soup. "But I stuffed it full of Old Sty, which is my father's brand of pipe tobacco. I also sneaked a few matches." He smirked proudly. "See? I do think of everything."

With a struggle, we mounted Crazy Horse. My left foot kicked into an eggbeater handle. So did Soup's right. The mule didn't move.

Soup, seated behind me, said, "Rob, you steer. And back here in the rear, I'll control the speed."

"How?" I asked, as would any curious Wahooligan.

"Like *this!*" Soup's heels kicked Crazy Horse.

Forward she bolted like a rocket gone mad.

"Steer," hollered Soup.

"I can't."

"Why not?" he was yelling.

"Because *you*, the genius who remembers every-thing, forgot to make a bridle. We don't have any *reins*."

It didn't matter. A dozen reins wouldn't steer Crazy Horse or slow her down. I knew nothing about mule riding except for the fact that I wanted to bail out. My fingers locked into the mule's mane, what little there was of it. Only stubble.

Soup kicked her again.

"Don't do that," I yelped.

"We need speed," said Soup. "So we can make a dramatic entrance at the pageant, and you'll impress Norma Jean."

Never did I realize that a mule could gallop so fast. Feathers were blowing out of my underwear, one after another. Eyes closed, I prayed that Crazy Horse knew where she was going. I hoped either to the pageant or to the hospital.

Lucky for us, it was a short trip.

The three of us arrived at the battle scene. Wrestlers punching lumberjacks. And lumberjacks socking wrestlers. A cheering crowd. Even the lady wrestlers seemed to be fighting among themselves.

Would anyone notice *us*?

Somebody noticed! Only one person. The onlooker who had brought a personal weapon, plus a supply of ammunition. Soup and I knew who it was when Janice's first cherry bomb exploded.

BAM.

Several events happened.

Crazy Horse, with her front hoofs braced, screeched to a sudden stop. Soup struck a match and fired the peace pipe. Women screamed and men fainted. My bare foot slipped out of my egg-beater. Janice Riker loaded her slingshot with another cherry bomb, then pulled back the twin strips of red inner-tube rubber, taking aim. Right at me.

A big bucket of cherry bombs stood between Janice's feet. An arsenal. Her depot of demonic destruction.

"Me Spreadeagle," Soup was hollering. "Lonely Skunk and I attack with a pipe of peace." He puffed out a rancid cloud of smoke that smelled oddly like his mother's sink drain. I coughed.

"Soup," I said, gagging, "get rid of that awful thing. Before I upchuck Old Sty all over Crazy Horse. Throw it to a redcoat or a patriot. Throw it away!"

He threw it.

I watched Soup's smoking piece of pipe sailing end over end, high in the air above the crowd. Down it came. *Clank!* It hit a rock sidewalk, then hopped (as though it had eyes) into a hiding place, totally out of sight. The burning pipe disappeared into the muzzle of Big Mouth, our town cannon, the one that was overloaded with an entire keg of gunpowder. A few sparks popped out of the big mouth of Big Mouth.

"Oh, no," I managed to say.

The citizens of Learning saw it all. Speechless in terror, they stood in place, wondering what would happen next. It happened. Big Mouth's big moment.

KAA-BBBOOOOOOOMMMMM.

Most of Vermont blew up, as well as parts of New York and New Hampshire. My ears went completely deaf. Yet, through the thick cloud of black smoke, I could somehow see Janice's cherry bomb pop straight up for about a hundred feet.

Down it fell. Into her bucket of bombs.

WWHHHHHHHHAAAAAAAAMMMMM-MMM.

Our entire battle scene detonated into a frantic finale of frenzy . . . with one exception. Crazy Horse stood motionless. She seemed to enjoy watching Janice blow herself up, and brayed an approval.

HEE HAAWWW.

"A mule remembers," I recalled Mr. Sanity Wacko's telling us.

One by one, Janice's cherry bombs all exploded. The world flooded with fire. Red rockets glared. Bombs were bursting in air. July was jubilant. Our town became a Star-Spangled Banner of rural patriotism.

No pageant ever ended in so booming a blast.

Both the British redcoats and the New England patriots, fearful of their lives, surrendered to the Last of the Wahooligans. Actors fell to the ground, prayed, or waved white hankies of retreat. Children laughed or threw up.

As the smoke began to clear, people were coughing less, so I presumed the worst was over. But nobody's right all the time. Certainly not me. That's when I saw it begin, unable to believe what I was watching. As far as I could recall, it had never budged before.

Big Mouth moved!

I pointed. "Soup," I said, "look at our cannon. It's starting to roll backward."

"Miss Kelly was right," he mumbled.

Right then, both of us were remembering what Miss Kelly had taught in science class: "For every force there is a counterforce. For example, the kick of a gun. When a cannon is fired, it tends to recoil backward."

Back the cannon rolled, gaining speed down the hill of our village green. Big Mouth seemed to have her sights set in reverse . . . aiming exactly at the gray granite statue of our founder, Mr. Ability Learning. Big Mouth rolled fast, then faster, her awesome weight being accentuated by gravitational pull. The crowd held its collective breath.

"Disability," someone yelled, "you'd better duck."

On rolled Big Mouth.

"Oh, dear me," I heard another voice whisper. "Big Mouth just might *damage* our statue."

KAA-WAACCCCCKKKKKO.

Damage wasn't the word. It was *destroy*, or *demolish*. Following impact, little remained of Mr. Learning's fleeing form except a pile of dust. Citizens wailed and wept. Because they had truly witnessed Disability's Final Disaster. But then a voice spoke up.

"Good neighbors," said Mr. Sanity Wacko, "let's not allow a minor mishap to dampen our day. I'm near a hundred year old. And in my will, I'm leaving money to the town for a new statue, one that *ain't* been politically corrected. It'll be a fair monument to a fine man . . . Mr. Ability Learning."

Suddenly they did it.

Everyone clapped their hands and hooted happy hurrahs. Two large fellows, one a local lumberjack and the other a visiting wrestler, hoisted Mr. Sanity Wacko atop their burly shoulders, then proudly paraded him among the crowd.

Looking at me, Soup grinned. "Rob, old sport, we certain did do it. We brought dignity and respect to Ability Learning and to Sanity Wacko."

Everyone in town wanted to congratulate Mr. Wacko, pat him on the back, or shake his hand. At last they set him on his feet again. Right beside the four of us. So there we stood, the five Wahooligans:

Chief Sitting Duck, Bold Beaver, Wet Blanket, Spreadeagle, and me (Lonely Skunk).

Soup was cheering.

"Rob," he yelled, "we are the true victors. Instead of all those predictable cowboy movies where the Indians always lose . . . we Wahooligans *won!*"

And to make our Battle Victory Day even more enjoyable, Crazy Horse stood taller than ever, because she was standing on Janice Riker.

Someone started to sing *God Bless America,* and everyone joined in. Voices rose to the sky. The song was perfect because it was entirely vocal, without the so-called talents of the Blunt Instruments. It made me happy to see Miss Boland smile as she was singing. For her, Battle Victory Day had somehow turned out to be a success.

The song ended.

Behind me, I heard the deep rumble of Sheriff Blood. "Who was responsible for tossing that torch into the cannon? I'm out to collar that rascal."

Soup silently melted away in the crowd.

I was alone. But then I heard a soft, sweet voice. "Rob." I turned to greet her with my rust-covered smile. "Rob," asked Norma Jean Bissell, "did you really write the pageant? It was wonderful. And so very romantic. Soup told everyone that you wrote the entire script."

My chest swelled. "Single-handed," I told her. "And perhaps a bit underhanded." As I smiled, I was praying that my one remaining chicken feather wouldn't forsake my underwear. "You probable noticed us in the battle scene," I added. "Soup and I were an eagle and a skunk. And I did wash this morning. Do I still smell like a cow?"

"No," said Norma Jean, "and you don't smell like an eagle."

Lonely Skunk grinned.